AN OVERPRAISED SEASON

Each of the ten stories in this collection presents some aspect of the emotional confrontation between the young and other people. A boy experiences adult hypocrisy for the first time and finds it more horrifying than personal failure. The family romances which have been familiar to Mattie from her early childhood suddenly take on a completely new meaning when she begins to think of having a romance of her own. An English lesson on Shakespeare is also a mental conflict between the teacher and the students. A boy suddenly sees his dull father as having once been attractive to an attractive woman.

The collection, which includes work by Doris Lessing, Kurt Vonnegut, John Updike, Elizabeth Taylor and H.E. Bates, stands as a brilliant illumination of Samuel Butler's observation that 'youth is like spring, an overpraised season'.

An Overpraised Season

◆◆◆

TEN STORIES SELECTED BY CHARLOTTE ZOLOTOW

◆◆◆

THE BODLEY HEAD
LONDON

British Library Cataloguing
in Publication Data
An Overpraised season: ten stories of youth.
1. Short stories, English   2. English fiction – 20th century
I. Zolotow, Charlotte
823'.01'08 [FS]   PR1309.S5
ISBN 0-370-30758-5

Copyright © 1973 by Charlotte Zolotow
All rights reserved
Printed in Finland for
The Bodley Head Ltd
32 Bedford Square, London WC1B 3EL
by Werner Söderström Oy
First published by Harper & Row Inc., New York, 1973
First published in Great Britain 1974
Reprinted and bound in this format 1987

For Paul Zindel
who knows all seasons

To me it seems that youth is
like spring, an overpraised season—
delightful if it happens to be a favoured one,
but in practice very rarely favoured and
more remarkable, as a general rule, for
biting east winds than genial breezes.

—Samuel Butler, *The Way of All Flesh*

Contents

An
Overpraised
Season

THE LIE
Kurt Vonnegut, Jr.

It was early springtime. Weak sunshine lay cold on old gray frost. Willow twigs against the sky showed the golden haze of fat catkins about to bloom. A black Rolls-Royce streaked up the Connecticut Turnpike from New York City. At the wheel was Ben Barkley, a black chauffeur.

"Keep it under the speed limit, Ben," said Doctor Remenzel. "I don't care how ridiculous any speed limit seems, stay under it. No reason to rush—we have plenty of time."

Ben eased off on the throttle. "Seems like in the springtime she wants to get up and go," he said.

"Do what you can to keep her down—O.K.?" said the doctor.

"Yes, sir!" said Ben. He spoke in a lower voice to the thirteen-year-old boy who was riding beside him, to Eli Remenzel, the doctor's son. "Ain't just people and animals feel good in the springtime," he said to Eli. "Motors feel good too."

"Um," said Eli.

"Everything feel good," said Ben. "Don't you feel good?"

"Sure, sure I feel good," said Eli emptily.

"Should feel good—going to that wonderful school," said Ben.

That wonderful school was the Whitehill School for Boys, a private preparatory school in North Marston, Massachusetts. That was where the Rolls-Royce was bound. The plan was that Eli would enroll for the fall semester, while his father, a member of the class of 1939, attended a meeting of the Board of Overseers of the school.

"Don't believe this boy's feeling so good, doctor," said Ben. He wasn't particularly serious about it. It was more genial springtime blather.

"What's the matter, Eli?" said the doctor absently. He was studying blueprints, plans for a thirty-room addition to the Eli Remenzel Memorial Dormitory—a building named in honor of his great-great-grandfather. Doctor Remenzel had the plans draped over a walnut table that folded out of the back of the front seat. He was a massive, dignified man, a physician, a healer for healing's sake, since he had been born as rich as the Shah of Iran. "Worried about something?" he asked Eli without looking up from the plans.

"Nope," said Eli.

Eli's lovely mother, Sylvia, sat next to the doctor, reading the catalogue of the Whitehill School. "If I were you," she said to Eli, "I'd be so excited I could hardly stand it. The best four years of your whole life are just about to begin."

"Sure," said Eli. He didn't show her his face. He gave her only the back of his head, a pinwheel of coarse brown hair above a stiff white collar, to talk to.

"I wonder how many Remenzels have gone to White-hill," said Sylvia.

"That's like asking how many people are dead in a cemetery," said the doctor. He gave the answer to the old joke, and to Sylvia's question too. "All of 'em."

"If all the Remenzels who went to Whitehill were numbered, what number would Eli be?" said Sylvia. "That's what I'm getting at."

The question annoyed Doctor Remenzel a little. It didn't seem in very good taste. "It isn't the sort of thing you keep score on," he said.

"Guess," said his wife.

"Oh," he said, "you'd have to go back through all the records, all the way back to the end of the eighteenth century, even, to make any kind of a guess. And you'd have to decide whether to count the Schofields and the Haleys and the MacLellans as Remenzels."

"Please make a guess—" said Sylvia, "just people whose last names were Remenzel."

"Oh—" The doctor shrugged, rattled the plans. "Thirty maybe."

"So Eli is number thirty-one!" said Sylvia, delighted with

the number. "You're number thirty-one, dear," she said to the back of Eli's head.

Doctor Remenzel rattled the plans again. "I don't want him going around saying something asinine, like he's number thirty-one," he said.

"Eli knows better than that," said Sylvia. She was a game, ambitious woman, with no money of her own at all. She had been married for sixteen years, but was still openly curious and enthusiastic about the ways of families that had been rich for many generations.

"Just for my own curiosity—not so Eli can go around saying what number he is," said Sylvia, "I'm going to go wherever they keep the records and find out what number he is. That's what I'll do while you're at the meeting and Eli's doing whatever he has to do at the Admissions Office."

"All right," said Doctor Remenzel, "you go ahead and *do* that."

"I will," said Sylvia. "I think things like that are interesting, even if you don't." She waited for a rise on that, but didn't get one. Sylvia enjoyed arguing with her husband about her lack of reserve and his excess of it, enjoyed saying, toward the end of arguments like that, "Well, I guess I'm just a simple-minded country girl at heart, and that's all I'll ever be, and I'm afraid you're going to have to get used to it."

But Doctor Remenzel didn't want to play that game. He

found the dormitory plans more interesting.

"Will the new rooms have fireplaces?" said Sylvia. In the oldest part of the dormitory, several of the rooms had handsome fireplaces.

"That would practically double the cost of construction," said the doctor.

"I want Eli to have a room with a fireplace, if that's possible," said Sylvia.

"Those rooms are for seniors."

"I thought maybe through some fluke—" said Sylvia.

"What kind of fluke do you have in mind?" said the doctor. "You mean I should demand that Eli be given a room with a fireplace?"

"Not *demand*—" said Sylvia.

"Request firmly?" said the doctor.

"Maybe I'm just a simple-minded country girl at heart," said Sylvia, "but I look through this catalogue, and I see all the buildings named after Remenzels, look through the back and see all the hundreds of thousands of dollars given by Remenzels for scholarships, and I just can't help thinking people named Remenzel are entitled to ask for a little something extra."

"Let me tell you in no uncertain terms," said Doctor Remenzel, "that you are not to ask for anything special for Eli—not anything."

"Of course I won't," said Sylvia. "Why do you always think I'm going to embarrass you?"

"I don't," he said.

"But I can still think what I think, can't I?" she said.

"If you have to," he said.

"I have to," she said cheerfully, utterly unrepentant. She leaned over the plans. "You think those people will like those rooms?"

"What people?" he said.

"The Africans," she said. She was talking about thirty Africans who, at the request of the State Department, were being admitted to Whitehill in the coming semester. It was because of them that the dormitory was being expanded.

"The rooms aren't for them," he said. "They aren't going to be segregated."

"Oh," said Sylvia. She thought about this awhile, and then she said, "Is there a chance Eli will have to have one of them for a roommate?"

"Freshmen draw lots for roommates," said the doctor. "That piece of information's in the catalogue too."

"Eli?" said Sylvia.

"H'm?" said Eli.

"How would you feel about it if you had to room with one of those Africans?"

Eli shrugged listlessly.

"That's all right?" said Sylvia.

Eli shrugged again.

"I guess it's all right," said Sylvia.

"It had better be," said the doctor.

The Rolls-Royce pulled abreast of an old Chevrolet, a car in such bad repair that its back door was lashed shut with clothesline. Doctor Remenzel glanced casually at the driver, and then, with sudden excitement and pleasure, he told Ben Barkley to stay abreast of the car.

The doctor leaned across Sylvia, rolled down his window, yelled to the driver of the old Chevrolet, "Tom! Tom!"

The man was a Whitehill classmate of the doctor. He wore a Whitehill necktie, which he waved at Doctor Remenzel in gay recognition. And then he pointed to the fine young son who sat beside him, conveyed with proud smiles and nods that the boy was bound for Whitehill.

Doctor Remenzel pointed to the chaos of the back of Eli's head, beamed that his news was the same. In the wind blustering between the two cars they made a lunch date at the Holly House in North Marston, at the inn whose principal business was serving visitors to Whitehill.

"All right," said Doctor Remenzel to Ben Barkley, "drive on."

"You know," said Sylvia, "somebody really ought to write an article—" And she turned to look through the back window at the old car now shuddering far behind. "Somebody really ought to."

"What about?" said the doctor. He noticed that Eli had slumped way down in the front seat. "Eli!" he said sharply.

17

"Sit up straight!" He returned his attention to Sylvia.

"Most people think prep schools are such snobbish things, just for people with money," said Sylvia, "but that isn't true." She leafed through the catalogue and found the quotation she was after.

"*The Whitehill School operates on the assumption,*" she read, "*that no boy should be deterred from applying for admission because his family is unable to pay the full cost of a Whitehill education. With this in mind, the Admissions Committee selects each year from approximately 3000 candidates the 150 most promising and deserving boys, regardless of their parents' ability to pay the full $2200 tuition. And those in need of financial aid are given it to the full extent of their need. In certain instances, the school will even pay for the clothing and transportation of a boy.*"

Sylvia shook her head. "I think that's perfectly amazing. It's something most people don't realize at all. A truck-driver's son can come to Whitehill."

"If he's smart enough," he said.

"Thanks to the Remenzels," said Sylvia with pride.

"And a lot of other people too," said the doctor.

Sylvia read out loud again: "*In 1799, Eli Remenzel laid the foundation for the present Scholarship Fund by donating to the school forty acres in Boston. The school still owns twelve of those acres, their current evaluation being $3,000,000.*"

"Eli!" said the doctor. "Sit up! What's the matter with you?"

Eli sat up again, but began to slump almost immediately, like a snowman in hell. Eli had good reason for slumping, for actually hoping to die, or disappear. He could not bring himself to say what the reason was. He slumped because he knew he had been denied admission to White-hill. He had failed the entrance examinations. Eli's parents did not know this, because Eli had found the awful notice in the mail and had torn it up.

Doctor Remenzel and his wife had no doubts what-soever about their son's getting into Whitehill. It was in-conceivable to them that Eli could not go there, so they had no curiosity as to how Eli had done on the examina-tions, were not puzzled when no report ever came.

"What all will Eli have to do to enroll?" said Sylvia, as the black Rolls-Royce crossed the Rhode Island border.

"I don't know," said the doctor. "I suppose they've got it all complicated now with forms to be filled out in quadruplicate, and punch-card machines and bureaucrats. This business of entrance examinations is all new, too. In my day a boy simply had an interview with the head-master. The headmaster would look him over, ask him a few questions, and then say, 'There's a Whitehill boy.' "

"Did he ever say, 'There isn't a Whitehill boy'?" said Sylvia.

"Oh, sure," said Doctor Remenzel, "if a boy was impossibly stupid or something. There have to be standards. There have always been standards. The African boys have to meet the standards, just like anybody else. They aren't getting in just because the State Department wants to make friends. We made that clear. Those boys had to meet the standards."

"And they did?" said Sylvia.

"I suppose," said Doctor Remenzel. "I heard they're all in, and they all took the same examination Eli did."

"Was it a hard examination, dear?" Sylvia asked Eli. It was the first time she'd thought to ask.

"Um," said Eli.

"What?" she said.

"Yes," said Eli.

"I'm glad they've got high standards," she said, and then she realized that this was a fairly silly statement. "Of course they've got high standards," she said. "That's why it's such a famous school. That's why people who go there do so well in later life."

Sylvia resumed her reading of the catalogue again, opened out a folding map of "The Sward," as the campus of Whitehill was traditionally called. She read off the names of features that memorialized Remenzels—the Sanford Remenzel Bird Sanctuary, the George MacLellan Remenzel Skating Rink, the Eli Remenzel Memorial Dormitory, and then she read out loud a quatrain printed on one corner of the map:

"When night falleth gently
Upon the green Sward,
It's Whitehill, dear Whitehill,
Our thoughts all turn toward."

"You know," said Sylvia, "school songs are so corny when you just read them. But when I hear the Glee Club sing those words, they sound like the most beautiful words ever written, and I want to cry."

"Um," said Doctor Remenzel.

"Did a Remenzel write them?"

"I don't think so," said Doctor Remenzel. And then he said, "No—Wait. That's the *new* song. A Remenzel didn't write it. Tom Hilyer wrote it."

"The man in that old car we passed?"

"Sure," said Doctor Remenzel. "Tom wrote it. I remember when he wrote it."

"A scholarship boy wrote it?" said Sylvia. "I think that's awfully nice. He *was* a scholarship boy, wasn't he?"

"His father was an ordinary automobile mechanic in North Marston."

"You hear what a democratic school you're going to, Eli?" said Sylvia.

Half an hour later Ben Barkley brought the limousine to a stop before the Holly House, a rambling country inn twenty years older than the Republic. The inn was on the edge of the Whitehill Sward, glimpsing the school's rooftops and spires over the innocent wilderness of the Sanford Remenzel Bird Sanctuary.

Ben Barkley was sent away with the car for an hour and a half. Doctor Remenzel shepherded Sylvia and Eli into a familiar, low-ceilinged world of pewter, clocks, lovely old woods, agreeable servants, elegant food and drink.

Eli, clumsy with horror of what was surely to come, banged a grandmother clock with his elbow as he passed, made the clock cry.

Sylvia excused herself. Doctor Remenzel and Eli went to the threshold of the dining room, where a hostess welcomed them both by name. They were given a table beneath an oil portrait of one of the three Whitehill boys who had gone on to become President of the United States.

The dining room was filling quickly with families. What every family had was at least one boy about Eli's age. Most of the boys wore Whitehill blazers—black, with pale-blue piping, with Whitehill seals on their breast pockets. A few, like Eli, were not yet entitled to wear blazers, were simply hoping to get in.

The doctor ordered a Martini, then turned to his son and said, "Your mother has the idea that you're entitled to special privileges around here. I hope you don't have that idea too."

"No, sir," said Eli.

"It would be a source of the greatest embarrassment to me," said Doctor Remenzel with considerable grandeur, "if I were ever to hear that you had used the name Remenzel as though you thought Remenzels were something special."

"I know," said Eli wretchedly.

"That settles it," said the doctor. He had nothing more to say about it. He gave abbreviated salutes to several people he knew in the room, speculated as to what sort of party had reserved a long banquet table that was set up along one wall. He decided that it was for a visiting athletic team. Sylvia arrived, and Eli had to be told in a sharp whisper to stand when a woman came to a table.

Sylvia was full of news. The long table, she related, was for the thirty boys from Africa. "I'll bet that's more colored people than have eaten here since this place was founded," she said softly. "How fast things change these days!"

"You're right about how fast things change," said Doctor Remenzel. "You're wrong about the colored people who've eaten here. This used to be a busy part of the Underground Railroad."

"Really?" said Sylvia. "How exciting." She looked all about herself in a birdlike way. "I think everything's exciting here. I only wish Eli had a blazer on."

Doctor Remenzel reddened. "He isn't entitled to one," he said.

"I know that," said Sylvia.

"I thought you were going to ask somebody for permission to put a blazer on Eli right away," said the doctor.

"I wouldn't do that," said Sylvia, a little offended now. "Why are you always afraid I'll embarrass you?"

"Never mind. Excuse me. Forget it," said Doctor Remenzel.

Sylvia brightened again, put her hand on Eli's arm, and looked radiantly at a man in the dining-room doorway. "There's my favorite person in all the world, next to my son and husband," she said. She meant Dr. Donald Warren, headmaster of the Whitehill School. A thin gentleman in his early sixties, Doctor Warren was in the doorway with the manager of the inn, looking over the arrangements for the Africans.

It was then that Eli got up abruptly, fled the dining room, fled as much of the nightmare as he could possibly leave behind. He brushed past Doctor Warren rudely, though he knew him well, though Doctor Warren spoke his name. Doctor Warren looked after him sadly.

"I'll be damned," said Doctor Remenzel. "What brought that on?"

"Maybe he really *is* sick," said Sylvia.

The Remenzels had no time to react more elaborately, because Doctor Warren spotted them and crossed quickly to their table. He greeted them, some of his perplexity about Eli showing in his greeting. He asked if he might sit down.

"Certainly, of course," said Doctor Remenzel expansively. "We'd be honored if you did. Heavens."

"Not to eat," said Doctor Warren. "I'll be eating at the long table with the new boys. I would like to talk, though." He saw that there were five places set at the table. "You're expecting someone?"

"We passed Tom Hilyer and his boy on the way," said Doctor Remenzel. "They'll be along in a minute."

"Good, good," said Doctor Warren absently. He fidgeted, looked again in the direction in which Eli had disappeared.

"Tom's boy will be going to Whitehill in the fall?" said Doctor Remenzel.

"H'm?" said Doctor Warren. "Oh—yes, yes. Yes, he will."

"Is he a scholarship boy, like his father?" said Sylvia.

"That's not a polite question," said Doctor Remenzel severely.

"I beg your pardon," said Sylvia.

"No, no—that's a perfectly proper question these days," said Doctor Warren. "We don't keep that sort of information very secret any more. We're proud of our scholarship boys, and they have every reason to be proud of themselves. Tom's boy got the highest score anyone's ever got on the entrance examinations. We feel privileged to have him."

"We never *did* find out Eli's score," said Doctor Remenzel. He said it with good-humored resignation, without expectation that Eli had done especially well.

25

"A good strong medium, I imagine," said Sylvia. She said this on the basis of Eli's grades in primary school, which had ranged from medium to terrible.

The headmaster looked surprised. "I didn't tell you his scores?" he said.

"We haven't seen you since he took the examinations," said Doctor Remenzel.

"The letter I wrote you—" said Doctor Warren.

"What letter?" said Doctor Remenzel. "Did we get a letter?"

"A letter from me," said Doctor Warren, with growing incredulity. "The hardest letter I ever had to write."

Sylvia shook her head. "We never got any letter from you."

Doctor Warren sat back, looking very ill. "I mailed it myself," he said. "It was definitely mailed—two weeks ago."

Doctor Remenzel shrugged. "The U.S. mails don't lose much," he said, "but I guess that now and then something gets misplaced."

Doctor Warren cradled his head in his hands. "Oh, dear—oh, my, oh, Lord," he said. "I was surprised to see Eli here. I wondered that he would want to come along with you."

"He didn't come along just to see the scenery," said Doctor Remenzel. "He came to enroll."

"I want to know what was in the letter," said Sylvia.

26

Doctor Warren raised his head, folded his hands. "What the letter said was this, and no other words could be more difficult for me to say: '*On the basis of his work in primary school and his scores on the entrance examinations, I must tell you that your son and my good friend Eli cannot possibly do the work required of boys at Whitehill.*' " Doctor Warren's voice steadied, and so did his gaze. " '*To admit Eli to Whitehill, to expect him to do Whitehill work,*' " he said, " '*would be both unrealistic and cruel.*' "

Thirty African boys, escorted by several faculty members, State Department men, and diplomats from their own countries, filed into the dining room.

And Tom Hilyer and his boy, having no idea that something had just gone awfully wrong for the Remenzels, came in, too, and said hello to the Remenzels and Doctor Warren gaily, as though life couldn't possibly be better.

"I'll talk to you more about this later, if you like," Doctor Warren said to the Remenzels, rising. "I have to go now, but later on—" He left quickly.

"My mind's a blank," said Sylvia. "My mind's a perfect blank."

Tom Hilyer and his boy sat down. Hilyer looked at the menu before him, clapped his hands and said, "What's good? I'm hungry." And then he said, "Say—where's your boy?"

"He stepped out for a moment," said Doctor Remenzel evenly.

"We've got to find him," said Sylvia to her husband.

"In time, in due time," said Doctor Remenzel.

"That letter," said Sylvia; "Eli knew about it. He found it and tore it up. Of course he did!" She started to cry, thinking of the hideous trap that Eli had caught himself in.

"I'm not interested right now in what Eli's done," said Doctor Remenzel. "Right now I'm a lot more interested in what some other people are going to do."

"What do you mean?" said Sylvia.

Doctor Remenzel stood impressively, angry and determined. "I mean," he said, "I'm going to see how quickly people can change their minds around here."

"Please," said Sylvia, trying to hold him, trying to calm him, "we've got to find Eli. That's the first thing."

"The first thing," said Doctor Remenzel quite loudly, "is to get Eli admitted to Whitehill. After that we'll find him, and we'll bring him back."

"But darling—" said Sylvia.

"No 'but' about it," said Doctor Remenzel. "There's a majority of the Board of Overseers in this room at this very moment. Every one of them is a close friend of mine, or a close friend of my father. If they tell Doctor Warren Eli's in, that's it—Eli's in. If there's room for all these other people," he said, "there's damn well room for Eli too."

He strode quickly to a table nearby, sat down heavily and began to talk to a fierce-looking and splendid old

28

gentleman who was eating there. The old gentleman was chairman of the board.

Sylvia apologized to the baffled Hilyers, and then went in search of Eli.

Asking this person and that person, Sylvia found him. He was outside—all alone on a bench in a bower of lilacs that had just begun to bud.

Eli heard his mother's coming on the gravel path, stayed where he was, resigned. "Did you find out," he said, "or do I still have to tell you?"

"About you?" she said gently. "About not getting in? Doctor Warren told us."

"I tore his letter up," said Eli.

"I can understand that," she said. "Your father and I have always made you feel that you had to go to Whitehill, that nothing else would do."

"I feel better," said Eli. He tried to smile, found he could do it easily. "I feel so much better now that it's over. I tried to tell you a couple of times—but I just couldn't. I didn't know how."

"That's my fault, not yours," she said.

"What's father doing?" said Eli.

Sylvia was so intent on comforting Eli that she'd put out of her mind what her husband was up to. Now she realized that Doctor Remenzel was making a ghastly mistake. She didn't want Eli admitted to Whitehill, could see what a cruel thing that would be.

29

She couldn't bring herself to tell the boy what his father was doing, so she said, "He'll be along in a minute, dear. He understands." And then she said, "You wait here, and I'll go get him and come right back."

But she didn't have to go to Doctor Remenzel. At that moment the big man came out of the inn and caught sight of his wife and son. He came to her and to Eli. He looked dazed.

"Well?" she said.

"They—they all said no," said Doctor Remenzel, very subdued.

"That's for the best," said Sylvia. "I'm relieved. I really am."

"Who said no?" said Eli. "Who said no to what?"

"The members of the board," said Doctor Remenzel, not looking anyone in the eye. "I asked them to make an exception in your case—to reverse their decision and let you in."

Eli stood, his face filled with incredulity and shame that were instant. "You what?" he said, and there was no childishness in the way he said it. Next came anger. "You shouldn't have done that!" he said to his father.

Doctor Remenzel nodded. "So I've already been told."

"That isn't done!" said Eli. "How awful! You shouldn't have."

"You're right," said Doctor Remenzel, accepting the scolding lamely.

"Now I *am* ashamed," said Eli, and he showed that he was.

Doctor Remenzel, in his wretchedness, could find no strong words to say. "I apologize to you both," he said at last. "It was a very bad thing to try."

"Now a Remenzel *has* asked for something," said Eli.

"I don't suppose Ben's back yet with the car?" said Doctor Remenzel. It was obvious that Ben wasn't. "We'll wait out here for him," he said. "I don't want to go back in there now."

"A Remenzel asked for something—as though a Remenzel were something special," said Eli.

"I don't suppose—" said Doctor Remenzel, and he left that sentence unfinished, dangling in the air.

"You don't suppose what?" said his wife, her face puzzled.

"I don't suppose," said Doctor Remenzel, "that we'll ever be coming here any more."

HOW LOVE CAME TO GRANDMOTHER
Merrill Joan Gerber

My elder daughter has long outgrown "The Three Bears," "Rumpelstiltskin," and even "Rapunzel"—and these days when she is in bed with the flu or a cold (today it is a strep throat), and when she has tired of her current jigsaw puzzle, her movie magazines, and the uninventive guppies in the stringy bowl on the night table, she asks me to tell her a story "from the old days."

"Tell me again how you met Daddy," she says. We always have a little furtive smile together when she says that, because the story is a secret between us, and one Daddy is never allowed to hear. If he ever comes into the room during the telling, Mattie expires in giggles, and little Clara, who is usually busy in the middle of the floor with her dominoes or Rubber Robots, laughs her little baby laugh as though she is more in on the joke than anyone, and poor Daddy goes away puzzled, but always in good-humored indignation. At the moment, Clara is napping and Daddy is at work.

So I begin. "In the old days, when I was a young girl, your grandfather, who is my daddy, had a little clock shop in downtown Brooklyn."

Mattie snuggles down under the blankets with a delighted smile now that she has captured my attention for probably the rest of the morning, because we both know what this story leads to: how Grandmother met Grandfather, and how Great-grandmother met Great-grandfather.

But it is fun for all of us, I don't mind, there is something deeply satisfying about pouring our very unimportant family history into these eager little ears, and to imagine Mattie telling it sweetly to her children, and they to their children in the generations to come.

So I automatically touch Mattie's forehead with my lips, disregarding her impatient shrug, and, noting that her temperature is, if not normal, at least no higher than it was, I go on with the love story I have told so often, remembering the sound of the story now better than the events of it.

"The clock shop was on Hanson Place, just down from the Long Island Railroad Station, and you always knew when you were getting near the shop because right on the corner was the Williamsburg Savings Bank, with a great round clock on its steeple. Your grandfather always set the clocks in his shop by the bank clock. On Saturdays, when there was no school, I went along with him to work to help in the store. My job was to wind all the clocks and watches in the window, and set them all at the right time, and dust out the showcase and sweep the floor. Most of the time your grandfather sat at the back of the store over a little wooden table, repairing watches. A great bright bulb shone down on the table, and Father wore big black magnifying glasses up around his forehead, which he slid down over his eyes when he had to look at a very tiny watch part.

"One day your daddy came along, and looked in the window. He was very young and handsome (and very skinny then, too—though you'd never believe it), and he carried a violin case under his arm. He was on his way to his violin teacher's house for his lesson, which he took every Saturday morning. He looked in the window for a long time, and I looked at him, my heart beating very fast, and finally, with a very puzzled expression on his face, he came into the store and said to me: 'Excuse me, but could you tell me what time it is? I'm on the way to a music lesson, and I'm afraid I'm late.' I thought it was just a big excuse, because there were more watches in one square foot of that window than in half of Switzerland, and I thought your daddy, seeing me through the window, had been unable to resist my charms, and had to come in and meet me.

"But just then your grandfather's voice boomed out from the back—'Young man, Eastern Standard Time is written on the face of every clock in that window!' 'Yes sir,' said your daddy, 'but every clock says something different.'

"Father and I both ran out in front and looked in the window, and sure enough, every single clock told a different time. 'Ruthie,' your grandfather said to me, severely, 'didn't you wind the clocks this morning?' And of course I hadn't, because I was too busy mooning around and dreaming of a handsome man like your daddy, and wishing he would come along and carry me off on his white horse."

Mattie giggles. "You mean they didn't have cars, it was so long ago?" I make a face at her, and she sticks out her tongue at me, and then goes on to finish the story in her little singsong. "And then Daddy stopped in to see you every Saturday when he went to his violin lesson because he was sorry he had gotten you in trouble, and then he fell in love with you, and when you finished school he married you."

"Something like that."

"Boy, it's a good thing he did," Mattie says, "—else where would I be?"

"You might be someone else," I tell her. "A movie actress, or a famous ice-skating star . . ."

". . . or a ditch digger," she adds. After a minute she says, "Mother, how do you suppose I'll meet my husband?"

"Oh, you never know. It doesn't matter really. It's always nice, however you do."

"Maybe I'll never get married," she says. "I'm going on twelve and I've never even had a date."

"I wouldn't give yourself up for lost yet, sweetie. Most people get married if they want to."

"Aunt Jenny wanted to. What about her?"

Aunt Jenny is my mother's sister, actually Mattie's *great*-aunt, who is now seventy-three, living out her lonely, petty life in a cooperative apartment building for old people in Coney Island.

"Aunt Jenny is another story. She never tried to meet men. She stayed cooped up in the house all the time like a nun. Even when the family was desperate for money after your great-grandfather died, she wouldn't budge out of the house to get a job."

"She seemed very nice when she was here Christmas," Mattie remarks.

"Well, she's nice when she wants to be," I say, hearing my voice take on a defensive tone, "but how do you explain the way she acted when Great-grandfather died, and your grandmother had to go out and support the whole family, while Aunt Jenny wouldn't lift a finger? You know that story, don't you?"

"I know that story," Mattie says. Her voice is flat, and she is twisting a ringlet around her finger, not looking at me.

"Well, was that a nice thing to do?" I say. "She was perfectly capable. She could have helped carry the load a little. Instead my mother had to do it all."

"Aunt Jenny had very bad pimples. She was embarrassed to go out of the house."

"How do you know?"

"She told me that at Christmas. She told me her face was so awful, she cried about it every day."

"It wasn't that bad at all, Mattie. My mother told me it was all in Jenny's mind."

"Well, I like her," Mattie says.

We are both silent, and the friendly morning seems rather ruined, somehow.

Finally I say, "Time for your medicine. Do you want a little orange juice?"

"No medicine yet," Mattie states. "First tell me again about how Great-grandmother met Great-grandfather. I like that one."

She is cheery again, so I try to be.

"Well, my grandmother, who is Great-grandmother to you, was born in Poland. That's a little country across the ocean—"

"I know where it is," Mattie interrupts. "We had it in Geography."

"Anyway, she wanted to come to America—everyone did in those days—so from the time she was twelve years old, just a bit older than you, she worked as a housekeeper for a lady in Poland, and saved all her money for boat fare."

"And she didn't have to go to school because in those days only the men went to school to study the Torah, right?"

"Right."

"And her mother didn't mind that she went to work because things were different in those days. Right?"

"Right."

"Would you let *me* quit school and go to work?"

"No. Things are different these days."

Mattie smiles crookedly. "Okay, tell me about the herring."

"When your great-grandmother was eighteen, she had finally saved up enough money to come to this country, so she collected her few clothes, and her mother (that's your great-*great*-grandmother) packed her enough food for the trip, and she left for America."

"Do you know how my great-great-grandmother met *her* husband?" Mattie asks.

"No," I say. "Things get lost that far back."

"Okay, go on."

"She went steerage class, because that's the way you had to go if you had very little money, and she had to travel in the bottom of the ship, under the deck, and they had no beds or bunks and had to sleep on blankets on the floor. A lot of the passengers were dirty and had lice on their bodies, and Great-grandmother wore a *babushka* on her head, hoping it would protect her hair from the lice, because she knew if any got on her, she would have to pour kerosene in her hair and then have her head shaved when the ship landed in America.

"They had a very rough crossing, and the ship rolled for days and days, and Great-grandmother got very seasick. She couldn't eat any of the food her mother had packed for her, and she got weaker and weaker, but every time she unwrapped a cracker or a piece of cheese, she just got more nauseous, and had to stuff it right back in the bag before she threw up.

"On the third day of not eating anything, she fainted, and a young man, also traveling steerage, helped her to sit up, and asked her if there were anything he could do to help. 'I haven't eaten in three days,' she said, 'and the only thing I can imagine swallowing is a piece of lox. That's the only thing in the world that I think I could eat.' 'Would herring do?' said the young man. '*Herring*!' cried Great-grandmother. 'A whole ocean full of fish, and the nearest herring is in Poland.' 'The nearest herring is in my pocket,' said the young man—and he pulled it out, and fed it to her, and she gave him all her crackers and cheese and fruit, and he gave her the rest of his herrings, and they ate together all the way to America."

"And got married when they got here," said Mattie.

"Correct."

40

"And then they had your mother, and your mother married your father and they had you, and you married Daddy and had me."

"Correct again. How about your medicine now?"

"Okay, but only if you promise to tell me the story of Grandmother right afterward."

"It's a deal." I go into the kitchen for the capsule, and check Clara in her crib on the way back. Mattie swallows the pill with a terrible face and a shudder.

This telling of tales seems less delightful today than it has ever been. Mattie is not listening to me the way she used to. She is interrupting more, and being too critical. She is watching my face peculiarly, with the same expression she had one night a few years ago when I had finished telling her "Snow White and the Seven Dwarfs" for about the millionth time. With that funny look on her face, she had turned her head up to me and said, "That's all a bunch of hogwash, isn't it, Mother?"

Now she settles down under the blankets again, and says, "This one used to be my favorite one of all—about the long hair."

"Isn't it your favorite any more?" I ask.

"We'll have to see," she says cryptically.

"Well—" I begin. "This is the story of how my mother met my father, which is the story of how your grandmother met your grandfather. As you know, your great-grandfather died when Grandmother was a very young girl."

"That's the man with the herring," says Mattie.

"And your great-grandmother was not very well—"

"From eating all that lox," says the child.

"So Grandmother had to go out and work to support Aunt Jenny and Great-grandmother."

"And Aunt Jenny stayed home and wouldn't work because she was lazy," says Mattie in the tone she uses to reel off the timetables.

"That's right. She was very lazy. She would stay in bed till noon, and Grandmother got up at six and went to work all the way to Manhattan on the subway, and Aunt Jenny stayed at home reading love poems and making valentines."

"For who?"

"How should I know for who? For the man-in-the-moon, I suppose. When Grandmother asked her if she would wash and iron some clothes because she had to wear a clean dress to work every day, Jenny complained and grumbled all week. One night, during the summer, Jenny decided to have a party, although she hardly knew a soul because she never set foot out of the house. She called up a few girls she knew and asked one of them if her boyfriend could bring along an extra boy for her.

"When Grandmother came home from work that night, the party was going on, even though it was very late.

Grandmother had worked overtime, and was tired, and a friend of hers had been kind enough to drive her home from work. She said goodnight to him outside, and came into the house. She walked through the bright living room where everyone was, then through the kitchen and up the back stairs to her bedroom. She put on her nightgown, took all the pins out of her mane of brown hair, and brushed it one hundred strokes over each shoulder. Then she decided to sneak down to the kitchen to have a glass of milk before she went to sleep. She went down the back stairs into the kitchen, and pouring the milk in a glass, stepped outside onto the dark back porch to sit on the wicker glider and drink it.

"And there was Grandfather. Sitting on the old rocker, smoking his pipe in the dark—the smell of summer roses coming up from the backyard. Grandmother said 'Excuse me' because she hadn't meant to come out and scare him like that, and Grandfather said to excuse *him*, he really should be in there with all the people, but he didn't like parties much, and he had been dragged along as an extra man, and he didn't feel very extra. He just wanted to sit by himself till his friend was ready to go home.

"Even though he was shy, he told Grandmother she had the prettiest, softest hair he'd ever seen, and she laughed and said how could he see in the dark—and he laughed too, and soon they were laughing so hard together that Grandmother spilled milk down the front of her nightgown, and just as Grandfather was leaning over to offer her his handkerchief, Aunt Jenny came out on the porch and Grandmother decided she had better go up to bed. And the next evening Grandfather came by and took Grandmother walking, and soon they had set the date."

I take a deep breath and look at Mattie. "The end," I say.

She looks neither amused nor delighted. She is making an odd face. Finally she says, "Poor Aunt Jenny."

"What has Aunt Jenny got to do with it?"

"No one ever married her. She never had any fun. If Clara ever does to me what Grandmother did to Aunt Jenny, I'll kill her."

"What on earth are you talking about, Mattie?"

"That's not what happened at all. All that stuff about just coming down for a glass of milk."

"What do you mean?" We eye each other as enemies.

"Aunt Jenny at Christmas told me the same story. Only it wasn't the same. I said to her 'Tell me the story about how Grandma met Grandpa' and she told me *some*thing, but it sure wasn't what *you* always tell me."

"What was it?"

"Well, first of all, Aunt Jenny had all these pimples, and she cried every time she looked in the mirror, she was so miserable. And Grandmother was beautiful. Aunt Jenny said she was the most beautiful girl anyone could

44

imagine, with a skin like lilies and hair like a waterfall. Aunt Jenny had to stay home all the time with Great-grandmother, while Grandmother went out to work every day and wore pretty clothes, and met different people, and had lots of boyfriends. All Aunt Jenny did was take out the garbage and do Grandmother's dirty laundry, and cry her eyes out. Once she tried to get a job working in a bakery, and the lady there told her that with a face like hers no one would buy the bread she touched."

Mattie stops, and reaches for a Kleenex on the night table. "What a lousy life she has," says the child.

"What *else* did she have to tell you?"

"Well, about this party. Aunt Jenny was so lonely she couldn't stand it anymore, and she thought maybe if she could meet a nice boy and let him get to know her, he would see she wasn't as awful as she looked. So she called up three of the girls she knew who all had boyfriends, and invited them to a party, and asked one of them if her boyfriend could bring along a boy for Aunt Jenny to meet. So they had this party, and someone brought along Grandfather for her to meet, and he was very nice to her and polite and she almost thought he liked her, until Grandmother came home from a date, her lipstick all smeared up and everything. She marched right through the living room on her high heels, showing off her pretty legs, and with her nose in the air, too

45

stuck-up even to say hello to anyone. And she had this big wavy bun of hair that caught the light, Aunt Jenny said, and shined like silk. And Grandfather kept staring at her.

"As soon as Grandmother disappeared, Grandfather just left Aunt Jenny flat, and went out on the back porch by himself. In a little while Grandmother came downstairs, in her nightgown. Imagine," says Mattie, ". . . in her *nightgown!*"

"*I* told you that," I say, in shock both at my child and at what she has to say to me.

"You didn't say a *sheer* nightgown."

"Is that what Aunt Jenny told you?"

"Yes. Anyway, Grandmother walked around in this nightgown, with her hair hanging down past her waist and swinging every which way, and everyone stopped and looked at her. She went into the kitchen and the light shined right through her nightgown."

"Mattie, that's my *mother* you're talking about."

"Yes," she says. "Thank God *you're* not that way."

She pulls another Kleenex and blows her nose.

"Then Grandmother went out on the porch where Aunt *Jenny's* date was, and she was half-naked nearly, and she stayed and talked to him most of the night, and when Aunt Jenny finally got the courage to go out there, they were pawing each other."

"Where did you get that *language*?" I cry.

"All the kids say that."

46

"Well, you are not to speak that way."

"What's a word that means the same thing, then?"

"Never mind. No such thing ever happened. Aunt Jenny was filling you up with a lot of fairy tales. She's just a malicious, jealous old woman."

"Well, she has a right to be, having a sexy, stinky sister like that, who had all the fun."

"You *believe* her?"

"Well, if Grandmother stole Aunt Jenny's only chance for a husband when *she* could have married anyone else in the world, that's pretty crummy."

"It's not true."

"If Clara ever does that to me, I'll kill her. I already get pimples on my face, sometimes, and Clara's hair is much prettier than mine. No one will marry me and I'll end up going crazy."

"You leave Clara alone. If your grandmother were alive, you could ask her yourself. It's easy for Jenny to spread her lies with my mother not here to dispute them."

"I like her. She's my favorite aunt."

"She'll never set foot in this house again!"

"Then I'll go see her when I grow up."

"Go ahead then. Do what you please."

I find in amazement I am about to cry, and worse, have visions of slapping my daughter senseless for what she is saying, and how she is saying it.

"Mattie," I say very quietly after a minute. "I loved my

47

mother very much. Do you understand that?"

"I'm tired of all these stories," Mattie says. "I think my hair is falling out from this disease I have. If I'm ever going to get married, I better take a nap and try to get well."

A RED-LETTER DAY

Elizabeth Taylor

The hedgerow was beaded with silver. In the fog the leaves dripped with a deadly intensity, as if each falling drop were a drop of acid.

Through the mist cabs came suddenly face to face with one another, passing and repassing between station and school. Backing into the hedges—twigs, withered berries striking the windows—the drivers leaned out to exchange remarks, incomprehensible to their passengers, who felt oddly at their mercy. Town parents especially shrank from this malevolent landscape—wastes of rotting cabbages, flint cottages with rakish privies, rubbish heaps, grey napkins dropping on clotheslines, the soil like plum cake. Even turning in at the rather superior school gates, the mossy stone, the smell of fungus, still dismayed them. Then, as the building itself came into view, they could see Matron standing at the top of the steps, fantastically white, shaming nature, her hands laid affectionately upon the shoulders of such boys as could not resist her. The weather was put in its place. The day would take its course.

Tory was in one of the last of the cabs. Having no man to exert authority for her, she must merely take her turn, standing on the slimy pavement, waiting for a car to come back empty. She stamped her feet, feeling the damp creeping through her shoes. When she left home she had thought herself suitably dressed; even for such an early hour her hat was surely plain enough? One after another she had tried on, and had come out in the end leaving hats all over the bed, so that it resembled a new grave with its mound of wreathed flowers.

One other woman was on her own. Tory eyed her with distaste. Her sons (for surely she had more than one? She looked as if she had what is often called a teeming womb; was like a woman in a pageant symbolizing maternity), her many sons would never feel the lack of a father, for she was large enough to be both to them. Yes, Tory thought, she would have them out on the lawn, bowling at them by the hour, coach them at mathematics, oil their bats, dubbin their boots, tan their backsides (she was working herself up into a hatred of this woman, who seemed to be all that she herself was not)—one love affair in her life, or, rather, mating. "She has probably eaten her husband now that her childbearing days are over. He would never have dared to ask for a divorce, as mine did." She carried still her "mother's bag"—the vast thing which, full of napkins, bibs, bottles of orange juice, accompanies babies out to tea. Tory wondered what was in it now. Sensible things: a Bradshaw, ration books, a bag of biscuits, large clean handerchiefs, a tablet of soap, and aspirins.

A jolly manner. "I love young people. I feed on them," Tory thought spitefully. The furs on her shoulders made her even larger; they clasped paws across her great authoritative back like hands across the ocean. Tory lifted her muff to hide her smile.

Nervous dread made her feel fretful and vicious. In *her* life all was frail, precarious; emotions fleeting, relationships fragmentary. Her life with her husband had suddenly loosened and dissolved, her love for her son was painful, shadowed by guilt—the guilt of having nothing solid to offer, of having grown up and forgotten, of adventuring still, away from her child, of not being able to resist those emotional adventures, the tenuous grasping after life; by the very look of her attracting those delicious secret glances, glimpses, whispers, the challenge, the excitement—not deeply sexual, for she was flirtatious; but not, she thought, watching the woman rearranging her furs on her shoulders, not a great featherbed of oblivion. Between Edward and me there is no premise of love, none at all, nothing taken for granted as between most sons and mothers, but all tentative, agonized. We are indeed

51

amateurs, both of us—no tradition behind us, no gift for the job. All we achieve is too hard come by. We try too piteously to please each other, and if we do, feel frightened by the miracle of it. I do indeed love him above all others. Above all others, but not exclusively.

Here a taxi swerved against the curb, palpitated as she stepped forward quickly, triumphantly, before Mrs. Hay-Hardy (whose name she did not yet know), and settled herself in the back.

"Could we share?" Mrs. Hay-Hardy asked, her voice confident, melodious, one foot definitely on the running board. Tory smiled and moved over much farther than was necessary, as if such a teeming womb could scarcely be accommodated on the seat beside her.

Shifting her furs on her shoulders, settling herself, Mrs. Hay-Hardy glanced out through the filming windows, undaunted by the weather, which would clear, she said, would lift. Oh, she was confident that it would lift by midday.

"One is up so early, it seems midday now," Tory complained.

But Mrs. Hay-Hardy had not risen until six, so that naturally it still seemed only eleven to her, as it was.

She will share the fare, Tory thought. Down to the last penny. There will be a loud and forthright women's argument. She will count out coppers and make a fuss.

This did happen. At the top of the steps Matron still

waited with the three Hay-Hardys grouped about her, and Edward, who blushed and whitened alternately with terrible excitement, a little to one side.

To this wonderful customer, this profitable womb, the headmaster's wife herself came into the hall. Her husband had sent her, instructing her with deft cynicism from behind his detective novel, himself one of those gods who rarely descend, except, like Zeus, in a very private capacity.

This is the moment I marked off on the calendar, Edward thought. Here it is. Every night we threw one of our pebbles out of the window—a day gone. The little stones had dropped back onto the gravel under the window, quite lost, untraceable, the days of their lives.

As smooth as minnows were Mrs. Lancaster's phrases of welcome; she had soothed so many mothers, mothered so many boys. Her words swam all one way in unison, but her heart never moved. Matron was always nervous; the results of her work were so much on the surface, so checked over. The rest of the staff could hide their inefficiency or shift their responsibility; she could not. If Mrs. Hay-Hardy cried, "Dear boy, your teeth!" to her first-born, as she did now, it was Matron's work she criticized, and Matron flushed. And Mrs. Lancaster flushed for Matron; and Derrick Hay-Hardy flushed for his mother.

Perhaps I am not a born mother, Tory thought, going down the steps with Edward. They would walk back to the Crown for lunch, she said. Edward pressed her arm as the taxi, bulging with Hay-Hardys, went away again down the drive.

"Do you mean you wanted to go with them?" she asked.

"No."

"Don't you like them?"

"No."

"But why?"

"They don't like me."

Unbearable news for any mother, for surely all the world loves one's child, one's only child? Doubt set in, a little nagging toothache of doubt. You *are* happy? she wanted to ask. "I've looked forward so much to this," she said instead. "*So* much."

He stared ahead. All round the gateposts drops of moisture fell from one leaf to another; the stone griffins were hunched up in misery.

"But I imagined it being a different day," Tory added. "Quite different."

"It will be nice to get something different to eat," Edward said.

They walked down the road towards the Crown as if they could not make any progress in their conversation until they had reached this point.

"You *are* warm enough at night?" Tory asked, when at last they were sitting in the hotel dining room. She could feel her question sliding away off him.

"Yes," he said absently and then, bringing himself back to the earlier, distant politeness, added, "Stifling hot."

"Stifling? But surely you have plenty of fresh air?"

"*I* do," he said reassuringly. "My bed's just under the window. Perishing. I have to keep my head under the bedclothes or I get earache."

"I am asking for all this," she thought. When the waiter brought her pink gin she drank it quickly, conscious that Mrs. Hay-Hardy, across the hotel dining room, was pouring out a nice glass of water for herself. She was so full of jokes that Tory felt she had perhaps brought a collection of them along with her in her shopping bag. Laughter ran round and round their table above the glasses of water. Edward turned once, and she glimpsed the faintest quiver under one eye, and an answering quiver on the middle Hay-Hardy's face.

She felt exasperated. Cold had settled in her; her mouth, her heart too, felt stiff.

"What would you like to do after lunch?" she asked.

"We could look round the shops," Edward said, nibbling away at his bread as if to keep hunger at arm's length.

The shops were in the Market Square. At the draper's the hats were steadily coming round into fashion again. "I could astonish everyone with one of these," Tory thought, setting her own hat right by her reflection in the window. Bales of apron print rose on both sides; a wax-faced little boy wore a stiff suit, its price ticket dangling from his yellow, broken fingers, his painted blue eyes turned mildly upon the street. Edward gave him a look of contempt and went to the shop door. Breathing on the glass in a little space among suspended bibs and jabots and parlourmaids' caps, he watched the cages flying overhead between cashier and counter.

The Hay-Hardys streamed by, heading for the open country.

Most minutely, Tory and Edward examined the draper's shop, the bicycle shop, the family grocer's. There was nothing to buy. They were just reading the postcards in the newsagent's window when Edward's best friend greeted them. His father, a clergyman, snatched off his hat and clapped it to his chest at the sight of Tory. When she turned back to the postcards she could see how unsuitable they were—jokes about bloomers, about twins; a great seaside world of fat men in striped bathing suits; enormous women trotted down to the sea's edge; crabs humorously nipped their behinds; farcical situations arose over bathing machines, and little boys had trouble with their water. She blushed.

The afternoon seemed to give a little sigh, stirred itself, and shook down a spattering of rain over the pavements. Beyond the Market Square the countryside, which had absorbed the Hay-Hardys, lowered at them.

"Is there anything you want?" Tory asked desperately, coveting the warm interiors of the shops.

"I could do with a new puncture outfit," Edward said.

They went back to the bicycle shop. My God, it's only three o'clock! Tory despaired, glancing secretly under her glove at her watch.

The Museum Room at the Guildhall was not gay, but at least there were Roman remains, a few instruments of torture, and half a mammoth's jawbone. Tory sat down on a seat among all the broken terra-cotta and took out a cigarette. Edward wandered away.

"No smoking, please," the attendant said, coming out from behind a case of stuffed deer.

"Oh, please!" Tory begged. She sat primly on the chair, her feet together, and when she looked up at him her violet eyes flashed with tears.

The attendant struck a match for her, and his hand, curving round it, trembled a little.

"It's the insurance," he apologized. "I'll have this later, if I may," and he put the cigarette she had given him very carefully in his breast pocket, as if it were a lock of her hair.

"Do you have to stay here all day long with these dull little broken jugs and things?" she asked, looking round.

He forgave her at once for belittling his life's work, only pointing out his pride, the fine mosaic on the wall.

"But floor should be lying down," she said naïvely— not innocently.

Edward came tiptoeing back.

"You see that quite delightful floor hanging up there?"

she said. "This gentleman will tell you all about it. My son adores Greek mythology," she explained.

"Your son!" he repeated, affecting gallant disbelief, his glance stripping ten or fifteen years from her. "This happens to be a Byzantine mosaic," he said and looked reproachfully at it for not being what it could not be. Edward listened grudgingly. His mother had forced him into similar situations at other times: in the Armoury of the Tower of London; once at Kew. It was as if she kindled in men a little flicker of interest and admiration which her son must keep fanned, for she would not. Boredom drew her away again, yet her charm must still hold sway. So now Edward listened crossly to the story of the Byzantine mosaic, as he had last holidays minutely observed the chasing on Henry VIII's breastplate, and in utter exasperation the holidays before that watched curlews through field glasses ("Edward is so very keen on birds") for the whole of a hot day while Tory dozed elegantly in the heather.

Ordinary days perhaps are better, Edward thought. Sinking down through him were the lees of despair, which must at all costs be hidden from his mother. He glanced up at every clock they passed and wondered about his friends. Alone with his mother, he felt unsafe, wounded and wounding; saw himself in relation to the outside world, oppressed by responsibility. Thoughts of the future, and even, as they stood in the church porch to shelter from another little gust of rain, of death, seemed to alight on him, brushed him, disturbed him, as they would not do if he were at school, anonymous and safe.

Tory sat down on a seat and read a notice about missionaries, chafing her hands inside her muff while all her bracelets jingled softly.

Flapping, black, in his cassock, a clergyman came hurrying through the graveyard, between the dripping umbrella trees. Edward stepped guiltily outside the porch as if he had been trespassing.

"Good afternoon," the vicar said.

"Good afternoon," Tory replied. She looked up from blowing the fur of her muff into little divisions, and her smile broke warmly, beautifully, over the dark afternoon.

Then, "The weather—" both began ruefully, broke off and hesitated, then laughed at each other.

It was wonderful; now they would soon be saying good-bye. It was over. The day they had longed for was almost over—the polite little tea among the chintz, the wheel-back chairs of the Copper Kettle; Tory frosty and imperious with the waitresses, and once Edward beginning, "Father—" at which she looked up sharply before she could gather together the careful indifference she always assumed at this name. Edward faltered. "He sent me a parcel."

"How nice!" Tory said, laying ice all over his heart. Her cup was cracked. She called the waitress. She could not drink tea from riveted china, however prettily painted. The waitress went sulkily away. All around them sat other little boys with their parents. Tory's bracelets tinkled as she clasped her hands tightly together and leaned forward. "And how," she asked brightly, indifferently, "how is your father's wife?"

Now the taxi turned in at the school gates. Suddenly the day withdrew; there were lights in the ground-floor windows. She thought of going back in the train, a lonely evening. She would take a drink up to her bedroom and sip it while she did her hair, the gas fire roaring in its white ribs, Edward's photograph beside her bed.

The Hay-Hardys were unloading at the foot of the steps; flushed from their country walk and all their laughter, they seemed to swarm and shout.

Edward got out of the taxi and stood looking up at Tory, his new puncture outfit clasped tightly in his hand. Uncertainly, awaiting a cue from her, he tried to begin his good-bye.

Warm, musky-scented, softly rustling, with the sound of her bracelets, the touch of her fur, she leaned and kissed him. "So lovely, darling!" she murmured. She had no cue to give him. Mrs. Hay-Hardy had gone into the school to have a word with Matron, so she must find her own way of saying farewell.

They smiled gaily as if they were greeting each other. "See you soon."

"Yes, see you soon."

"Good-bye, then, darling."

"Good-bye."

She slammed the door and, as the car moved off, leaned to the windows and waved. He stood there uncertainly, waving back, radiant with relief; then, as she disappeared round the curve of the drive, ran quickly up the steps to find his friends and safety.

TOTAL STRANGER
James Gould Cozzens

Clad in a long gray duster, wearing a soft gray cap, my father, who was short and strong, sat bolt upright. Stiffly, he held his gauntleted hands straight out on the wheel. The car jiggled scurrying along the narrow New England country road. Sometimes, indignant, my father drove faster. Then, to emphasize what he was saying, and for no other reason, he drove much slower. Though he was very fond of driving, he drove as badly as most people who had grown up before there were cars to drive.

"Well," I said, "I can't help it."

"Of course you can help it!" my father snorted, adding speed. His severe, dark mustache seemed to bristle a little. He had on tinted sunglasses, and he turned them on me.

"For heaven's sake, look what you're doing!" I cried. He looked just in time, but neither his dignity nor his train of thought was shaken. He continued: "Other boys help it, don't they?"

"If you'd just let me finish," I began elaborately. "If you'd just give me a chance to—"

"Go on, go on," he said. "Only don't tell me you can't help it! I'm very tired of hearing—"

"Well, it's mostly Mr. Clifford," I said. "He has it in for me. And if you want to know why, it's because I'm not one of his gang of bootlickers, who hang around his study to bum some tea, every afternoon practically." As I spoke, I could really feel that I would spurn an invitation so dangerous to my independence. The fact that Mr. Clifford rarely spoke to me except to give me another hour's detention became a point in my favor. "So, to get back at me, he tells the Old Man—"

"Do you mean Doctor Holt?"

"Everyone calls him that. Why shouldn't I?"

"If you were a little more respectful, perhaps you wouldn't be in trouble all the time."

"I'm not in trouble all the time. I'm perfectly respectful. This year I won't be in the dormitory any more, so Snifty can't make up a lot of lies about me."

My father drove dashing past a farmhouse in a billow of dust and flurry of panic-struck chickens. "Nonsense!" he said. "Sheer nonsense! Doctor Holt wrote that after a long discussion in faculty meeting he was satisfied that your attitude—"

"Oh, my attitude!" I groaned. "For heaven's sake, a fellow's attitude! Of course, I don't let Snifty walk all over me. What do you think I am? That's what that means. It means that I'm not one of Snifty's little pets, hanging around to bum some tea."

"You explained about the tea before," my father said. "I don't feel that it quite covers the case. How about the other masters? Do they also expect you to come around and take tea with them? When they tell the headmaster that you make no effort to do your work, does that mean that they are getting back at you?"

I drew a deep breath in an effort to feel less uncomfortable. Though I was experienced in defending myself, and with my mother, could do it very successfully, there was a certain remote solemnity about my father which made me falter. From my standpoint, talking to my father was a risky business, since he was only interested in proved facts. From his standpoint, I had reason to know, my remarks would form nothing but a puerile exhibition of sorry nonsense. The result was that he avoided, as long as he could, these serious discussions, and I avoided, as long I could, any discussions at all.

I said laboriously, "Well, I don't think they told him that. Not all of them. And I can prove it, because didn't I get promoted with my form? What did I really flunk, except maybe algebra? I suppose Mr. Blackburn was the one who said it." I nodded several times, as though it confirmed my darkest suspicions.

My father said frigidly, "In view of the fact that your

grade for the year was forty-four, I wouldn't expect him to be exactly delighted with you."

"Well, I can tell you something about that," I said, ill at ease, but sufficiently portentous. "You can ask anyone. He's such a bum teacher that you don't learn anything in his courses. He can't even explain the simplest thing. Why, once he was working out a problem on the board, and I had to laugh, he couldn't get it himself. Until finally one of the fellows who is pretty good in math had to show him where he made a mistake even a first former wouldn't make. And that's how good he is."

My father said, "Now, I don't want any more argument. I simply want you to understand that this fall term will be your last chance. Doctor Holt is disgusted with you. I want you to think how your mother would feel if you disgrace her by being dropped at Christmas. I want you to stop breaking rules and wasting time."

He let the car slow down for emphasis. He gave me a look, at once penetrating and baffled. He could see no sense in breaking the simple, necessary rules of any organized society; and wasting time was worse than wrong, it was mad and dissolute. Time lost, he very well knew, can never be recovered. Left to himself, my father's sensible impulse would probably have been to give me a thrashing I'd remember. But this was out of the question, for my mother had long ago persuaded him that he, too, believed in reasoning with a child.

Looking at me, he must have found the results of reasoning as unimpressive as ever. He said, with restrained grimness: "And if you're sent home don't imagine that you can go back to the academy. You'll go straight into the public school and stay there. So just remember that."

"Oh, I'll remember all right," I nodded significantly. I had not spent the last two years without, on a number of occasions, having to think seriously about what I'd do if I were expelled. I planned to approach a relative of mine connected with a steamship company and get a job on a boat.

"See that you do!" said my father. We looked at each other with mild antagonism. Though I was still full of arguments, I knew that none of them would get me anywhere, and I was, as always, a little alarmed and depressed by my father's demonstrable rightness about everything. In my position, I supposed that he would always do his lessons, never break any rules, and probably end up a prefect, with his rowing colors and a football letter —in fact, with everything that I would like, if only the first steps toward them did not seem so dull and difficult. Since they did, I was confirmed in my impression that it was impossible to please him. Since it was impossible, I had long been resolved not to care whether I pleased him or not. Practice had made not caring fairly easy.

As for my father, surely he viewed me with much the same resentful astonishment. My mother was accustomed to tell him that he did not understand me. He must have been prepared to believe it; indeed, he must have wondered if he understood anything when he tried to reconcile such facts as my marks with such contentions as my mother's that I had a brilliant mind. At the moment he could doubtless think of nothing else to say, so he drove faster, as if he wanted to get away from the whole irksome matter; but suddenly the movement of the car was altered by a series of heavy, jolting bumps.

"Got a flat," I said with satisfaction and relief. "Didn't I tell you? Everybody knows those tires pick up nails. You can ask anybody."

My father edged the limping car to the side of the road. In those days you had to expect punctures if you drove any distance, so my father was not particularly put out. He may have been glad to get his mind off a discussion which was not proving very profitable. When we had changed the tire—we had demountable rims, which made it wonderfully easy, as though you were putting something over on a puncture—we were both in better spirits and could resume our normal, polite and distant attitudes. That is, what I said was noncommittal, but not impertinent; and what he said was perfunctory, but not hostile. We got into Sansbury at five o'clock, having covered one hundred and three miles, which passed at the time for a long, hard drive.

When my father drove me up to school, we always stopped at Sansbury. The hotel was not a good or comfortable one, but it was the only convenient place to break the journey. Sansbury was a fair-sized manufacturing town, and the hotel got enough business from traveling salesmen—who, of course, traveled by train—to operate in a shabby way something like a metropolitan hotel. It had a gloomy little lobby with rows of huge armchairs and three or four imitation-marble pillars. There were two surly bellboys, one about twelve, the other about fifty. The elevator, already an antique, was made to rise by pulling on a cable. In the dark dining room a few sad, patient, middle-aged waitresses distributed badly cooked food, much of it, for some reason, served in separate little dishes of the heaviest possible china. It was all awful.

But this is in retrospect. At the time I thought the hotel more pleasant than not. My father had the habit, half stoical, half insensitive, of making the best of anything there was. Though he acted with promptness and decision when it was in his power to change circumstances, he did not grumble when it wasn't. If the food was bad, favored by an excellent digestion, he ate it anyway. If his surroundings were gloomy and the company either boring to him or nonexistent, he did not fidget.

When he could find one of the novels at the moment seriously regarded, he would read it critically. When he couldn't, he would make notes on business affairs in a shorthand of his own invention which nobody else could read. When he had no notes to make, he would retire, without fuss or regret, into whatever his thoughts were.

I had other ideas of entertainment. At home I was never allowed to go to the moving pictures, for my mother considered the films themselves silly and cheap, and the theaters likely to be infested with germs. Away from home, I could sometimes pester my father into taking me. As we moved down the main street of Sansbury—my father serenely terrorizing all the rest of the traffic—I was watching to see what was at the motion-picture theater. To my chagrin, it proved to be Annette Kellerman in *A Daughter of the Gods*, and I could be sure I wouldn't be taken to that.

The hotel garage was an old stable facing the kitchen wing across a yard of bare dirt forlornly stained with oil. My father halted in the middle of it and honked his horn until finally the fifty-year-old bellboy appeared, scowling. While my father had an argument with him over whether luggage left in the car would be safe, I got out. Not far away there stood another car. The hood was up and a chauffeur in his shirt sleeves had extracted and spread out on a sheet of old canvas an amazing array of parts. The car itself was a big impressive landaulet with carriage lamps at the doorposts. I moved toward it and waited until the chauffeur noticed me.

"What's the trouble?" I inquired professionally.

Busy with a wrench, he grunted, "Cam shaft."

"Oh! How much'll she do?"

"Hundred miles an hour."

"Ah, go on!"

"Beat it," he said. "I got no time."

My father called me, and, aggrieved, I turned away, for I felt sure that I had been treated with so little respect because I had been compelled to save my clothes by wearing for the trip an old knickerbocker suit and a gray cloth hat with the scarlet monogram of a summer camp I used to go to on it. Following the aged bellboy through the passage toward the lobby, I said to my father, "Well, I guess I'll go up and change."

My father said, "There's no necessity for that. Just see that you wash properly, and you can take a bath before you go to bed."

"I don't see how I can eat in a hotel, looking like this," I said. "I should think you'd want me to look halfway respectable. I—"

"Nonsense!" said my father. "If you wash your face and hands, you'll look perfectly all right."

The aged bellboy dumped the bags indignantly and my father went up to the imitation-marble desk to register. The clerk turned the big book around and gave him a pen. I wanted to sign for myself, so I was standing close to him, watching him write in his quick, scratchy script, when suddenly the pen paused. He held his hand, frowning a little.

"Come on," I said, "I want to—"

"Now, you can just wait until I finish," he answered. When he had finished, he let me have the pen. To the clerk he said, "Curious coincidence! I used to know some-

71

one by that name." He stopped short, gave the clerk a cold, severe look, as though he meant to indicate that the fellow would be well advised to attend to his own business, and turned away.

The elevator was upstairs. While we stood listening to its creeping, creaky descent, my father said "Hm!" and shook his head several times. The lighted cage came into view. My father gazed at it a moment. Then he said "Hm!" again. It came shaking to a halt in front of us. The door opened and a woman walked out. Her eyes went over us in a brief, impersonal glance. She took two steps, pulled up short, and looked at us again. Then, with a sort of gasp, she said, "Why, Will!"

My father seemed to have changed color a little, but he spoke with his ordinary equability: "How are you, May? I had an idea it might be you."

She came right up to him. She put her hand on his arm. "Will!" she repeated. "Well, now, honestly!" She gave his arm a quick squeeze, tapped it and dropped her hand. "Will, I can't believe it! Isn't it funny! You know, I never planned to stop here. If that wretched car hadn't broken down—"

I was looking at her with blank curiosity, and I saw at once that she was pretty—though not in the sense in which you applied pretty to a girl, exactly. In a confused way, she seemed to me to look more like a picture—the sort of woman who might appear on a completed jigsaw puzzle, or on the back of a pack of cards. Her skin had a creamy, powdered tone. Her eyes had a soft, gay shine which I knew from unconscious observation was not usual in a mature face. Her hair was just so. Very faint, yet very distinct, too, the smell of violets reached me. Although she was certainly not wearing anything resembling evening dress, and, in fact, had a hat on, something about her made me think of my mother when she was ready to go to one of the dances they called assemblies, or of the mothers of my friends who came to dinner looking not at all as they usually looked. I was so absorbed in this feeling of strangeness—I neither liked it nor disliked it; it simply bewildered me—that I didn't hear anything until my father said rather sharply, "John! Say how do you do to Mrs. Prentice!"

"I can't get over it!" she was saying. She broke into a kind of bubbling laughter. "Why, he's grown up, Will! Oh, dear, doesn't it make you feel queer?"

Ordinarily, I much resented that adult trick of talking about you as if you weren't there, but the grown-up was all right, and she looked at me without a trace of the customary patronage; as though, of course, I saw the joke too. She laughed again. I would not have had the faintest idea why, yet I was obliged to laugh in response.

She asked brightly, "Where's Hilda?"

My father answered, with slight constraint, that my mother was not with us, that he was just driving me up to school.

Mrs. Prentice said, "Oh, that's too bad. I'd so like to see

her." She smiled at me again and said, "Will, I can't face that dreadful dining room. I was going to have something sent up. They've given me what must be the bridal suite." She laughed. "You should see it! Why don't we all have supper up there?"

"Capital!" my father said.

The word astonished me. I was more or less familiar with most of my father's expressions, and that certainly was not one of them. I thought it sounded funny, but Mrs. Prentice said, "Will, you haven't changed a bit! But then, you wouldn't. It comes from having such a wonderful disposition."

The aged bellboy had put our luggage in the elevator and shuffled his feet beside it, glowering at us: "Leave the supper to me," my father said. "I'll see if something fit to eat can be ordered. We'll be down in about half an hour."

In our room, my father gave the aged bellboy a quarter. It was more than a bellboy in a small-town hotel would ever expect to get, and so, more than my father would normally give, for he was very exact in money matters and considered lavishness not only wasteful but rather common, and especially bad for the recipient, since it made him dissatisfied when he was given what he really deserved. He said to me, "You can go in the bathroom first, and see that you wash your neck and ears. If you can get your blue suit out without unpacking everything else, change to that."

74

While I was splashing around I could hear him using the telephone. It did not work very well, but he must eventually have prevailed over it, for when I came out he had unpacked his shaving kit. With the strop hung on a clothes hook, he was whacking a razor up and down. Preoccupied, he sang, or rather grumbled, to himself, for he was completely tone-deaf: "I am the monarch of the sea, the ruler of the Queen's—"

The room where we found Mrs. Prentice was quite a big one, with a large dark-green carpet on the floor, and much carved furniture, upholstered where possible in green velvet of the color of the carpet. Long full glass curtains and green velvet drapes shrouded the windows, so the lights—in brass wall brackets and a wonderfully coiled and twisted chandelier—were on. There was also an oil painting in a great gold frame showing a group of red-trousered French soldiers defending a farmhouse against the Prussians—the type of art I liked most. It all seemed to me tasteful and impressive, but Mrs. Prentice said, "Try not to look at it." She and my father both laughed.

"I don't know what we'll get," my father said. "I did what I could."

"Anything will do," she said. "Will, you're a godsend. I was expiring for a cocktail, but I hated to order one by myself."

I was startled. My father was not a drinking man. At home I could tell when certain people were coming to dinner, for a tray with glasses and a decanter of sherry would appear in the living room about the time I was going upstairs, and a bottle of sauterne would be put in the icebox.

My mother usually had a rehearsal after the table was set, to make sure that the maid remembered how wine was poured.

Sometimes, when I was at the tennis club, my father would bring me into the big room with the bar and we would both have lemonades. I had never actually seen him drink anything else, so I had an impression that drinking was unusual and unnecessary. I even felt that it was reprehensible, since I knew that the man who took care of the garden sometimes had to be spoken to about it.

To my astonishment, my father said, as though it were the most natural thing in the world, "Well, we can't let you expire, May. What'll it be?"

She said, "I'd love a Clover Club, Will. Do you suppose they could make one?"

My father said, "We'll soon find out! But I think I'd better go down and superintend it myself. That bar looks the reverse of promising."

Left alone with Mrs. Prentice, my amazement kept me vaguely uncomfortable. I studied the exciting details of the fight for the farmhouse, but I was self-conscious, for

I realized that she was looking at me. When I looked at her, she was lighting a gold-tipped cigarette which she had taken from a white cardboard box on the table. She seemed to understand something of my confusion. She said, "Many years ago your father and I were great friends, John. After I was married, I went to England to live— to London. I was there until my husband died, so we didn't see each other. That's why we were both so surprised."

I could not think of anything to say. Mrs. Prentice tried again. "You two must have wonderful times together," she said. "He's lots of fun, isn't he?"

Embarrassed, I inadvertently nodded; and thinking that she had found the right subject, she went on warmly, "He was always the most wonderful swimmer and tennis player, and a fine cyclist. I don't know how many cups he took for winning the century run."

Of course, I had often seen my father play tennis. He played it earnestly, about as well as a strong but short-legged amateur who didn't have much time for it could. He was a powerful swimmer, but he did not impress me particularly, even when he swam, as he was fond of doing, several miles; for he never employed anything but a measured, monotonous breast stroke which moved him through the water with unbending dignity. It was very boring to be in the boat accompanying him across some Maine lake. I had no idea what a century run was, but I guessed it meant bicycling, so my confusion and amazement were all the greater. The fad for bicycling wasn't within my memory. I could as easily imagine my father playing tag or trading cigarette pictures as riding a bicycle.

Mrs. Prentice must have wondered what was wrong with me. She could see that I ought to be past the stage when overpowering shyness would be natural. She must have known, too, that she had a more than ordinary gift for attracting people and putting them at ease. No doubt, her failure with me mildly vexed and amused her.

She arose, saying, "Oh, I forgot! I have something." She swept into the room beyond. In a moment she came back with a box in her hands. I had stood up awkwardly when she stood up. She brought the box to me. It was very elaborate. A marvelous arrangement of candied fruits and chocolates filled it. I said, "Thank you very much." I took the smallest and plainest piece of chocolate I could see.

"You mustn't spoil your appetite, must you?" she said, her eyes twinkling. "You take what you want. We won't tell your father."

Her air of cordial conspiracy really warmed me. I tried to smile, but I didn't find myself any more articulate. I said again, "Thank you. This is really all I want."

"All right, John," she said. "We'll leave it on the desk there, in case you change your mind."

The door, which had stood ajar, swung open. In came my father, carrying a battered cocktail shaker wrapped in a napkin. He headed a procession made up of the young bellboy, with a folding table; the old bellboy, with a bunch of roses in a vase; and a worried-looking waitress, with a tray of silver and glasses and folded linen.

"Why, Will," Mrs. Prentice cried, "it's just like magic!"

My father said, "What it will be just like, I'm afraid, is the old Ocean House."

"Oh, oh!" Mrs. Prentice laughed. "The sailing parties! You know, I haven't thought of those—and those awful buffet suppers!"

"Very good," my father said, looking at the completed efforts of his procession. "Please try to see that the steak is rare, and gets here hot. That's all." He filled two glasses with pink liquid from the cocktail shaker. He brought one of them to Mrs. Prentice, and, lifting the other, said, "Well, May. Moonlight Bay!"

She looked at him, quick and intent. She began quizzically to smile. It seemed to me she blushed a little. "All right, Will," she said, and drank.

They were both silent for an instant. Then, with a kind of energetic abruptness, she said, "Lottie Frazer! Oh, Will, do you know, I saw Lottie a month or two ago."

I sat quiet, recognizing adult conversation, and knowing that it would be dull. I fixed my eyes on the battle picture. I tried to imagine myself behind the mottled stone wall with the French infantrymen, but constantly I heard Mrs. Prentice laugh. My father kept responding, but with an odd, light, good-humored inflection, as though he knew that she would laugh again as soon as he finished speaking. I could not make my mind stay on the usually engrossing business of thinking myself into a picture.

". . . you were simply furious," I heard Mrs. Prentice saying. "I didn't blame you."

My father said, "I guess I was."

"You said you'd break his neck."

They had my full attention, but I had missed whatever it was, for my father only responded, "Poor old Fred!" and looked thoughtfully at his glass. "So you're going back?"

Mrs. Prentice nodded. "This isn't really home to me. Becky and I are—well, I can hardly believe we're sisters. She disapproves of me so."

"I don't remember Becky ever approving of anything," my father said. "There's frankness for you."

"Oh, but she approved of you!" Mrs. Prentice looked at him a moment.

"I never knew it," said my father. "She had a strange way of showing it. I had the impression that she thought I was rather wild, and hanging would be too good—"

"Oh, Will, the things you never knew!" Mrs. Prentice shook her head. "And of course, the person Becky really couldn't abide was Joe. They never spoke to each other. Not even at the wedding." Mrs. Prentice gazed at me, but abstractedly, without expression. She started to look back to my father, stopped herself, gave me a quick little smile, and then looked. My father was examining his glass.

"Ah, well," he said, " 'there is a divinity that shapes our ends, roughhew them—' "

Mrs. Prentice smiled. "Do you still write poetry?" she asked.

My father looked at her as though taken aback. "No," he said. He chuckled, but not with composure. "And what's more, I never did."

"Oh, but I think I could say some of it to you."

"Don't," said my father. "I'm afraid I was a very pretentious young man." At that moment, dinner arrived on two trays under a number of big metal covers.

I thought the dinner was good, and ate all that was offered me; yet eating seemed to form no more than a pleasant, hardly noticed undercurrent to my thoughts. From time to time I looked at the empty cocktail glasses or the great box of candied fruits and chocolates. I stole glances at Mrs. Prentice's pretty, lively face. Those fragments of conversation repeated themselves to me.

Intently, vainly, I considered "century run," "Ocean House," "Moonlight Bay." I wondered about Fred, whose neck, it seemed, my father thought of breaking; about this Becky and what she approved of; and about the writing of poetry. My mother had done a good deal to acquaint me with poetry. She read things like "Adonais," the "Ode to a Nightingale," "The Hound of Heaven" to me; and though

I did not care much for them, I knew enough about poets to know that my father had little in common with pictures of Shelley and Keats. I had never seen a picture of Francis Thompson, but I could well imagine.

Thus I had already all I could handle; and though talk went on during the meal, I hardly heard what they were saying. My attention wasn't taken until Mrs. Prentice, pouring coffee from a little pot, said something about the car.

My father accepted the small cup and answered, "I don't know that it's wise."

"But I've just got to," she said. "I can't make the boat unless—"

"Well, if you've got to, you've got to," my father said. "Are you sure he knows the roads? There are one or two places where you can easily make the wrong turn. I think I'd better get a map I have and make it for you. It will only take a moment."

"Oh, Will," she said, "that would be such a help."

My father set his cup down and arose with decision. When we were alone, Mrs. Prentice got up too. As I had been taught to, I jumped nervously to my feet. She went and took the box from the desk and brought it to me again.

"Thank you very much," I stammered. I found another small plain piece of chocolate. "I'm going to put the cover on," she said, "and you take it with you."

I made a feeble protesting sound. I was aware that I ought not to accept such a considerable present from a person I did not know, but I realized that, with it, I was bound to be very popular on my arrival—at least, until the evening school meeting, when anything left would have to be turned in.

She could see my painful indecision. She set the box down. She gave a clear warm laugh, extended a hand and touched me on the chin. "John, you're a funny boy!" she said. My mother had sometimes addressed those very words to me, but with an air of great regret; meaning that the way I had just spoken or acted, while not quite deserving punishment, saddened her. Mrs. Prentice's tone was delighted, as though the last thing she meant to do was reprove me. "You don't like strangers to bother you, do you?"

The touch of her hand so astonished me that I hadn't moved a muscle. "I didn't think you were, at first," she said, "but you are! You don't look very much like him, but you can't imagine how exactly—" She broke into that delightful little laugh again. Without warning, she bent forward and kissed my cheek.

I was frightfully embarrassed. My instant reaction was a sense of deep outrage, for I thought that I had been made to look like a child and a fool. Collecting my wits took me a minute, however; and I found then that I was not angry at all. My first fear—that she might mean to imply that I was just a baby or a little boy—was too clearly unfounded. I was not sure just what she did mean, but part of it, I realized, was that I had pleased her somehow, that she had suddenly felt a liking for me, and that people she liked, she kissed.

I stood rigid, my face scarlet. She went on at once: "Will you do something for me, John? Run down and see if you can find my chauffeur. His name is Alex. Tell him to bring the car around as soon as he can. Would you do that?"

"Yes, Mrs. Prentice," I said.

I left the room quickly. It was only the second floor, so I found the stairs instead of waiting for the elevator. I went down slowly, gravely and bewildered, thinking of my father and how extraordinary it all was; how different he seemed, and yet I could see, too, that he really hadn't changed. What he said and did was new to me, but not new to him. Somehow it all fitted together. I could feel that.

I came into the lobby and went down the back passage and out to the yard. It was now lighted by an electric bulb in a tin shade over the stable door. A flow of thin light threw shadows upon the bare earth. The hood of the big landaulet was down in place, and the man was putting some things away. "Alex!" I said authoritatively.

He turned sharp, and I said: "Mrs. Prentice wants you to bring the car around at once." He continued to look at me a moment. Then he smiled broadly. He touched his cap and said, "Very good, sir."

When I got back upstairs, my father had returned. The old bellboy was taking out a couple of bags. After a moment Mrs. Prentice came from the other room with a coat on and a full veil pinned over her face and hat. "Thank you, John," she said to me. "Don't forget this." She nodded at the big box on the table. I blushed and took it.

"Aren't you going to thank Mrs. Prentice?" my father asked.

She said, "Oh, Will, he's thanked me already. Don't bother him."

"Bother him!" said my father. "He's not bothered. Why, I can remember my father saying to me, 'Step up here, sir, and I'll mend your manners!' And for less than not saying thank you. I'm slack, but I know my parental duties."

They both laughed, and I found myself laughing too. We all went out to the elevator.

In front of the hotel, at the bottom of the steps, the car stood. "Just see he follows the map," my father said. "You can't miss it." He looked at the sky. "Fine moonlight night! I wouldn't mind driving myself."

"Will," said Mrs. Prentice, "Will!" She took his hand in both of hers and squeezed it. "Oh, I hate to say good-by like this! Why, I've hardly seen you at all!"

"There," said my father. "It's wonderful to have seen you, May."

She turned her veiled face toward me. "Well, John! Have a grand time at school!"

I said, "Good-by, Mrs. Prentice. Thank you very much for the—"

The chauffeur held the door open and my father helped her in. There was a thick click of the latch closing. The chauffeur went around to his seat. We stood on the pavement, waiting while he started the engine. The window was down a little and I could hear Mrs. Prentice saying, "Good-by, good-by."

My father waved a hand and the car drew away with a quiet, powerful drone. It passed, the sound fading, lights glinting on it, down the almost empty street.

"Well, that's that!" said my father. He looked at me at last and said, "I think you might send a post card to your mother to tell her we got here all right."

I was feeling strangely cheerful and obedient. I thought fleetingly of making a fuss about the movies, but I decided not to. At the newsstand inside, my father bought me a post card showing a covered bridge near the town. I took it to one of the small writing tables by the wall.

"Dear Mother," I wrote with the bad pen, "arrived here safely." I paused. My father had bought a paper and, putting on his glasses, had settled in one of the big chairs. He read with close, critical attention, light shining on his largely bald head, his mustache drawn down sternly. I had seen him reading like that a hundred times, but tonight he did not look quite the same to me. I thought of Mrs. Prentice a moment, but when I came to phrase it, I could not think of anything to say. Instead, I wrote: "We drove over this bridge." I paused again for some time, watching my father read, while I pondered. I wrote: "Father and I had a serious talk. Mean to do better at school—"

Unfortunately, I never did do much better at school. But that year and the years following, I would occasionally try to, for I thought it would please my father.

CRIMSON RAMBLERS OF THE WORLD, FAREWELL

Jessamyn West

The October morning, when thirteen-year-old Elizabeth
Prescott opened her eyes, was sallow, like a faded suntan.
October mornings in Southern California can be many
different ways, but this was the way Elizabeth liked best,
sunshine remembered but not present. There had been just
enough rain in the night to stir up all the scents locked
in the dust by summer's heat and dryness. Hundreds of
smells, at the very least, sailed into her nose. It made her
feel a little crazy, so many smells she could not name:
castor bean she recognized, eucalyptus, wild tobacco, lico-
rice, off-bloom acacia, alfalfa, petunia, wet dirt, coffee
perking for breakfast. But most of the scents she could not
identify, sniff though she would.

Me, though, she thought triumphantly. I can smell me.
I'm a real hound-nose. Though it was really no test, con-
sidering her hour-long lathering with rose-geranium soap
before she had gone to bed. Her feet still felt withered

from last night's soaking in the foot tub. She lifted the covers to look at them: wrinkled but lily white, like the feet of a dead knight.

She let the covers drop and thought, I wish I had somebody to smile at. Oh boy, I wish I could wake up and smile at somebody and not stop smiling all day long. I wish I could wake up and someone would look into smiling eyes and say, "Another beautiful day, darling." Someone who knew that she was willing to get up, eager to dedicate her whole day to silence, hard work, and smiling. I wish it would be Mother and she wouldn't yell "Get up," or even whisper it. I wish I could smile a message at Mother and have it recognized; if a smile collided with a smile, whammo, bango, there'd be a big crack-up. Splinters of smiles, first crashing, then sparkling in the air like an explosion in a diamond mine, or maybe in a bombed mirror factory.

Well, I know someone, she thought, to smile at. I know Crimson Rambler Rice. Though she'd have to wait for school to smile at Crimson Rambler, and maybe by school time she wouldn't feel like smiling. At home things happened to stop smiles.

"I never knew anyone by the name of Rice who was any account," her mother had said.

Her mother had known lots of Rices, all amounting to less than a hill of beans. "And no puns intended either." So it was too much to expect that the one Rice her daughter had run across would be an exception to the rule.

"What does this Clarence Rice's father do?"

Elizabeth didn't know. What did that have to do with Clarence? Clarence? No one called him that. He had red hair and ran fast. When he'd started school in September, the kids had wanted to call him Red. He wouldn't let them.

"That's not my name."

"What's your name, Red?"

"Crimson Rambler."

"Why, Red?"

"Because my hair's crimson and I can ramble."

"Your hair's sure crimson, Red, but can you ramble?"

"Ramble round anything here."

So they had a track meet. Crimson Rambler (he said) Rice against the world. Everything on two feet he ran circles round. Dogs he kept up with (nobody had greyhounds at the Yorba Linda Grammar School). Ginny Todd's tomcat went past him like lightning past a hill. Then it climbed a tree.

"I'm no tree climber," Crimson Rambler said, "I never claimed that."

"How come you're a Crimson Rambler, then?" Elizabeth asked. "The crimson rambler is a climbing rose."

That decided the kids. If E. Prescott was against the Rambler, they were for him. She knew too much. No, that wasn't it. They didn't care how much she knew if only she'd keep it to herself. And she didn't, couldn't. Each morning on the way to school she rehearsed keeping it to herself. Then something like this would happen: Somebody who had *named* himself after a climber said he couldn't climb. So she had to point out the error.

"Crimson," the kids had said, just to show her, "you're a rambler, all right."

But Crimson Rambler didn't care how much she knew. He liked knowledge. He liked having his errors pointed out. He was a learner as well as a rambler. He liked her. He was the first boy who ever had—and shown it. He never said a loving word, but he didn't need to. He chose her first for every game; sat by her at lunchtime; when he passed the drawing paper he gave her more sheets than he gave anyone else; he never squirted anyone but her from the drinking fountain. And on Friday he had asked her to ride on Monday—this was Monday—on the handlebars of his bicycle. She had never ridden on any boy's handlebars, had never been asked before, had almost given up hoping.

Oh, Crimson Rambler! Thinking of his looks, she almost stopped smiling. They were too wonderful for smiles. Too ineluctable? Was that the word? Was it a *word*! Crimson Rambler's looks were one with all the stars and heavenly bodies and ancient gods. They were classical. When he smiled it was too sweet for the naked eye to endure. An expression at the corners of his mouth when he smiled said, All my strength and toughness and meanness (and he was strong and tough and mean) I am making sweet and gentle and quiet for you.

Oh Crimson Rambler Rice!

Who could she smile at now? Merv? Go smiling into Merv's room and say, "Brother, I forgive you everything"?

The trouble was she had nothing to forgive Merv. Mother was always saying, so that she and Howie could hear, "Merv is my favorite child." That was nothing to forgive Merv for. And there never *would* be anything to forgive Merv for and never any reason to smile at him either, because Merv wouldn't smile back. He wasn't mean or downcast, just too damn dead calm to smile.

Howie had something to forgive her for and she had something to forgive him for. "You'll never die of lockjaw," Howie had said to her.

That was something to forgive, and she was willing, but Howie was too mad at her to smile. She didn't blame Howie, though what she'd done had not been intended to hurt him. It had been intended to help him. The trouble was he didn't want help.

Mother had said, "Basil Cobb is teaching Howie dirty words." Howie was eight and Basil twelve.

"What kind of dirty words?"

"Never you mind. But you speak to him about it."

"Why can't Merv?"

"Merv wouldn't know what to say."

"I don't either."

"Something will come to you. It always does."

And it had. "Stop teaching my little brother dirty words."

"Like what, Movie Star Prescott?"

"Movie Star" was a thing she had to grin and bear. Because her name was Elizabeth and because she didn't look like a movie star, that's what mean kids called her.

"Like what?"

It was the first time in her life she'd been asked a question and had no answer. It was a humiliating thing to have to stand before a questioner wordless.

"Like what, Movie Star Prescott?"

She had no idea. She was ignorant as well as wordless.

"Like son of a bitch, Movie Star Prescott?"

So she slapped him. She knew it was a point of honor, when that was said, to fight. It was an aspersion cast upon your mother, and while you didn't have to fight for a brother, you had to fight for your mother. Otherwise you had a streak of yellow a yard wide. There were mothers, perhaps, you wouldn't want to fight for. But not hers.

Everywhere I look I see beauty, she thought; perhaps it was a defect of her eyes, like seeing double. Could both Crimson Rambler Rice and her mother be as beautiful as she thought them? Her mother had the two prettiest things in the world for a woman: little black curls at the back of her neck, falling down from the pulled-up knot of hair; and color in her face that swept back and forth from shell pink to deepest rose depending upon how glad or mad she was.

Her mother was very mad and very red when she heard of the slapping. "You have humiliated Howie," she said.

There was no disputing this.

"Here comes Sistie to button up your little pantsies, Howie baby," Basil would yell every time Howie came out of the boy's lavatory. There was no use denying that such talk was humiliating; just as there was no use expecting an early-morning smile from Howie either.

That left her father and her mother; and she knew she was already in bad with Father. Her hour-long bath in the kitchen last night had been, as much as anything, to wash away her troubles.

After supper her father had said, "Elizabeth, I'd like to have a little talk with you."

His voice, her full name, Mother's leaving the room had all told her that what Father had to say was serious. It was just dusk. He sat in his chair in the living room. His white shirt was visible but his dark trousers had disappeared into the big dark chair, and the big dark chair was disappearing in evening's shadow, going under like a sinking ship.

She stood before her father wanting to help him. It was not easy for her father to criticize her. She knew that. What came as natural as breathing to her mother hurt her father. She wanted to please her mother; but her father she wanted to help. She loved him, and almost the only way she had of showing it was being loving and dutiful with Mother. It was a wordless compact she and her father had. "If you love me, make your mother happy." That was what he said without words and what she without words agreed to. Father had recognized a fact: happiness, for him, was making Mother happy.

He gave everything to his wife, including his daughter and his daughter's love. She never kissed her father, hugged him, sat upon his knee as other daughters did. She never dared and he didn't want her to; not because he didn't like kissing and hugging *and* her, but because Mother would love him more if he sacrificed such pleasures —handed them over as a gift to her. So the way to show her father she loved him was to be cool to him and do loving things for Mother.

Only, time and again she failed: was cross, snappy, mean, selfish, critical, disobedient, and sometimes downright snarling-yelling mad. She loved her mother for the same reasons her father did, probably: for her funny jokes, her beautiful looks, her wonderful pies; and especially the excitement of living either in a cyclone or a storm cellar; one or the other all the time.

But what her father didn't see was that it was easier for him to be always calm and courteous, loving, in deed as in fact, to Mother than for her. Mother thought he was the most wonderful person in the world; she never slapped him, told him to shut up, asked him to do unreasonable things, or said to other people in his hearing, "He is not my favorite husband," the way she did with her when she said, "Liz is not my favorite child."

Her father asked a lot of his daughter. He asked her to be just as loving to her mother as he was to his wife. He asked her to forgo her love for him and present it as a gift to Mother. Since she really did love Mother, this required a love almost stronger than a human being could generate. And it made all her failures with Mother almost too heavy to bear. She failed two people when she failed Mother.

Last night her father had been resting his face in his hands. His eyes were out of sight. Only his Masonic ring caught lights and blinked a lodge greeting at her. In the silence, and knowing she had another double failure of some kind to face, her hands began to sweat and her stomach went slowly round and round, winding itself into a smaller and smaller knot to make room for a bigger and bigger sorrow.

"Elizabeth, don't answer me now. I want you to think about what I have to say for a while, then answer. Are you willing?"

Was she willing? She was willing to think until her brains steamed. Already the skin was tightening across her cheekbones and her mouth was widening and narrowing as she prepared herself to think. If thinking could undo the day before's yelling madness with Mother, she would think her eyeballs out of their sockets and break her eardrums with the pressure of cogitation.

"Tell me, Father," she said urgently. The engine of her brain was running hard, but it needed a direction in which to go.

"Elizabeth, you're such a fine girl, such a fine, bright, strong girl."

This was terrible: that her father thought he had to *say* these things.

"Your mother . . ." He couldn't go on.

"I love Mother."

"I know you do."

"But I argue, contradict, disobey, act scornful. . . ."

"Elizabeth, I think I'd be the happiest man on earth if you could get on better with your mother. I'd not ask for a thing more in life."

"I promise. I promise. . . ."

"Don't," her father urged. "Go think about it."

Thinking about it had been the whole trouble. If she could have spoken at once and without thinking, all she would have said was, "Oh, Father, I'll try to be better."

What she'd said later was the same thing exactly, only she'd had time while she was washing dishes to feel more and more. And the more she felt, the more impossible it was to come right out and say it. "Father, I'll try to be better." That's all it was, the same thing said in a fancy roundabout way. And, fool that she was, she'd even thought her father might enjoy the fanciness. She had wanted to bare her heart, make eternal promises, tell him of her steely resolutions; but not in so many words.

Thinking had told her how to say it—and not say it. And how to spare them both tears by roundaboutness.

She did a wonderful job on the dishes, dried her hands, combed her hair, and went to stand again before her father. He had vanished from sight now except for the white shirt, an iceberg on the dark water.

"Father?"

"Yes, Elizabeth."

"Father, I want you to know that whereas in the past you have had in this house a big, rough, unmannerly Airedale dog, growling and showing his teeth, he is now about to be replaced. . . ."

Her father interrupted her. "Elizabeth, what's this long story about dogs? What's it got to do with your attitude toward your mother?"

"Why, everything." But the story would explain that.

"Whereas," she started over, "you have had this big unmannerly Airedale in the house, in the future you will have a small gentle lap dog, quiet, well-behaved, gentle. . . ."

Her father had sprung to his feet as if stabbed.

"Stop it," he ordered. "If what you're trying to do is to give me a demonstration of what your mother has to put up with day in and day out, you've succeeded."

"Father, please let me . . ."

Her father fell back into his chair. "Enough is enough. Go play. Go study. Whatever you want. You haven't the least idea of what I was asking you."

And all the time the shoe was on the other foot. She

knew what he was asking and he didn't, but he wouldn't hear any more. All of him had gone from sight; the iceberg had sunk. Did they sink? No, melt. And Father was crying, she knew that; like something which thinks that because it is out of sight it can't be heard.

"Twenty-four hours a day of this," he said as she left. "No wonder your mother's nerves are frazzled."

"Frazzled?" her mother asked, coming from wherever she'd been listening to the conversation. "Who said anything about frazzled? And what's wrong with trying to make yourself clear by giving examples? The Bible does it all the time."

Elizabeth couldn't believe her ears. Mother saying that she was Biblical! And it was partly true. That was what was so astounding about Mother. She didn't skate around on the surface. She plunged in deep.

"The Bible's full of comparisons. Fig trees and lilies and houses built on sand. What's wrong with big dogs and little dogs, if they make the meaning clearer?"

Mother's arm around her was not a dead weight like other arms she'd had round her: uncles and aunts and such old worn-out huggers. Mother's arm was as alive as a king snake, warm and nonpoisonous, clasping her lovingly.

She snuggled into its curve. "Be this way forever," she prayed. Nine months ago, on the last day of the year, her mother sat up with her until the hikers came at midnight for the trip to Old Baldy. She hadn't asked her mother. Hadn't told her that the last hour of the old year, with snow on the mountain in the morning of the new year, was important. Mother *knew*. Her mother read her like a book. And sometimes clapped her shut like a book. And there was no way to stop that. She could only love the times she was read and pondered and understood.

She had taken her long bath to help her wash away her father's scolding; and her knowledge that her mother's arm that had cradled could be raised as quickly against her.

Things like that couldn't be washed away of course, but she had awakened smelling the October morning, thinking of Crimson Rambler and the bicycle ride, and smiling. And no one to smile at but herself. So she jumped out of bed and did so, in the mirror. It will be a better face, she thought, with time and suffering; though it would never be the small-boned, black-haired, pink-petaled face (the best kind of face, in her opinion) of her mother. But it was hers, and this was a day in her life and no one else's, and the day of her first ride on the handlebars of a boy's bicycle. No old twerp's; though whoever had asked her, she'd have accepted. She knew that. But fate had spared her, had made the first the best. Oh, Crimson Rambler Rice. Had he shined it, tied a ribbon on, lived Friday, Saturday, and Sunday waiting for this day? Was he smiling, too, as he got up, happy to see that it had rained in the night so that they could have a sweet-smelling dust-free ride?

She went to the window and looked out in the direction of the foothills where Crimson Rambler lived. The sallow light was pinker now. In the barley field meadowlarks were singing. A big unknown bird cleared the eucalyptus windbreak, then went up and up across the sky, straight and steady enough to be an airplane. No one had called her. From the kitchen, which was under her room—and which, as far as smells went, was practically in her room, her floor and the kitchen's ceiling being not only one and the same but with knotholes—the coffee smell came up stronger and stronger. Someone was up and cooking.

"The household is astir," she told herself. The words excited her. The smile went inward. She began her morning dance, which was mostly running and jumping; but the jumps were enormous flights that carried her half across the room. I'll invite Crimson Rambler for a ride on my wings in exchange for his bicycle courtesy.

Then she was suddenly tired as well as excited and lay down quickly on the floor and lifted the rug for a peek through the biggest knothole at life in the kitchen. Usually her father got up first and started things going: coffee, water for the oatmeal, oven heating for the toast. Sometimes he shaved at the kitchen sink. Every month or so she remembered to have a peek, and he had never known it, busy whistling, slicing bacon, having a trial cup of coffee. It was a secret she had, and the kitchen was her secret garden and the knothole her gate to enter.

On her stomach, comfortably full length, she lay quietly eye-spying her way into her secret garden. At first she saw no one, though there on the stove was the coffee-pot perking and the griddle smoking. Somewhere she heard splashing and by getting a little way from the knot-hole she was able to see her father, stark naked, standing at the kitchen sink having a kind of sponge bath from the washbasin there. He was rinsing off his private parts, and though her every intention was to back away fast, her eye fitted itself to that knothole like a ball bearing to a socket; she gazed as if this were the sight she had been created to see. Her father sloshed and whistled. It was her mother, coming into the kitchen with her sixth sense of just where to look to catch her daughter at her worst, who looked up immediately through the knothole and deep into her daughter's eye. She didn't say a word. They stared at each other as if their eyes had fallen into a lock which someone else would have to break. Then, still without speaking a word, her mother left the room.

She was standing, with the rug back down, when her mother entered the room. Her mother still had on her nightgown. Her black hair was hanging down her shoulders; her cheeks were burning.

"Do you do this very often?"

"Do what?"

"Don't spar with me, Peeping Tom. Look down into the kitchen through your peephole?"

"I've looked before."

"Does your father know it?"

"I don't think so."

"Have you seen him naked before?"

"No."

"But you've been waiting for your chance?"

"No, I haven't."

"You weren't backing away very fast."

"I was going to. I was getting ready to."

"What do you have to do to get ready to stop looking at your naked father?"

"I don't know."

"What kind of a girl do you think you are, up to such tricks?"

"I don't know."

"Do you think Merv would do a thing like that?"

"No."

"You're right. He wouldn't. Merv is a clean, natural, decent boy. He wouldn't stoop to spying on his naked mother. Or father. That is an unnatural act. You have heard of unnatural acts, haven't you?"

"Yes."

"Do you know what they are?"

"No."

"Spying on your naked father. That's an unnatural act."

"I didn't intend to."

"Flat on your face, eye glued to a peephole? Did somebody push you there?"

"No."

"No, no, no. Well, since you don't know, I'll tell you what you are. You are perverted. You have an unnatural interest in sex. And your own father! Your father was awake half the night worrying about you and your story to him about being some kind of a dog. Even though I tried to explain it. What kind of a daughter tells her father she's a dog? Tell me."

"Crazy, I guess."

"Do you know what a female dog is called?"

"Yes."

"What?"

"A bitch."

"Don't be one. I'm not going to tell your father about this. It would sicken him. But *I* know about it. And I am going to keep a close watch on you. Respect and obedience. That's all he wants from you. And with your tendencies, you'd better watch yourself when you get around *anything* with pants on."

At the bedroom door she said, "Wait until the rest of us have eaten. I don't think anyone would consider it a pleasure to eat with you this morning."

She didn't eat breakfast at all. She didn't go downstairs until her father had gone to work and her brothers had left for school.

When she came down the stairs her mother was waiting for her. "Elizabeth," she said, "I was upset, but what I said was for your own good. You're of an age now when you'll have to be careful. Guard yourself and your feelings."

Her mother put her arms around her and pressed her pink petal-cool cheek to hers, kissed her, as she sometimes did, on each eyelid, then stood in the door and waved until she went over the dip of the hill and out of sight.

The schoolyard was empty when she got there. She heard allegiance being pledged inside. Late was late, so she took an extra minute to inspect Crimson Rambler's bicycle; there it was on the rack, washed and polished and ready to go. Even the tires had been scrubbed. She tiptoed over to the bicycle and touched it. She felt daring. It was the next thing to touching Crimson Rambler himself. The bicycle was warm and smooth in the October sunlight, very bright, shining, and dust-free.

Even though Crimson Rambler Rice was two years older than she, over fifteen, actually, they were in the same room, and she had to walk in under his eyes. There was no use trying to smile. She wasn't happy that way any more, but she was excited, shaking even. She counted the steps to her desk and watched her feet to keep herself from staring at Crimson Rambler. But she saw him. She couldn't lower her eyelids far enough to hide even his clean sweat shirt or the comb marks in his freshly wet hair.

Arithmetic was first, and when Hank Simon passed the papers for this, he handed her a note, too. "Elizabeth" was printed on the outside in the big dashing way Crimson Rambler had. She opened it behind her arithmetic book.

It began "My sweetheart." That was all she read. "My sweetheart." That was really nauseating. She rose, surprising herself, and went with the note to the wastepaper basket at the front of the room. Then, looking straight at Crimson Rambler, she began to tear the note into tiny pieces. "Sweetheart"? Why, Crimson Rambler Rice, she thought, did you really think I could be anyone's sweetheart but mother's? I don't want a thing my mother doesn't give me, and anything anyone else gives me I'll give to her. Big old Crimson Rambler Rice, did you think you could win me away from my mother with your bicycle and silly notes? Did you think I'd fall for *anything* in pants? That shows how crazy you are, because people who've got any sense don't think much of girls like that. That shows you haven't got any standards to speak of, Crimson Rambler Rice, and I have.

The note, torn up, she let dribble in a little paper waterfall into the basket. Old silly Crimson Rambler and his "sweetheart"! Why, Mother, your merest loving glance means more to me than suggestive notes from boys.

Crimson Rambler stared at her, but she didn't care. By

the time the last of his note had fallen into the basket, she'd stopped trembling. She walked back toward her desk feeling happy to have made it up to her mother for all her earlier wicked thoughts, feeling strong and calm. Feeling like her father, calm, helpful, and devoted.

She stopped at the desk of Fione Quigley, a sweet little girl who didn't understand decimals. "Slide over, Fione," she said. "I'll help you with your arithmetic."

She put her arm around Fione's shoulder and whispered, "It's the same as fractions, only another way of saying it."

She looked to see if Crimson Rambler was watching. He was. She gave him a long square look and with eyes said, Farewell, Crimson Rambler Rice. Never try to tempt me again.

THE PLAYGROUND
Elizabeth Enright

The big heat-shrunken river swam through the city like a yellow serpent. Slowly it moved under the bridges and between the streets; past the penitentiary and the library and the post office and the great hotel where so many women wept the nights away from despair or simple boredom, for in those days, long ago, it took a whole half-year to kill a marriage. There the women were held, prisoners of time, writing letters, living for the mail, taking what they could from the bright Western days and the dry new country and the dry new friendships. The great sulky dappled stream with its bridges and feathered islands would always, for them, be part of a puzzled and unquiet memory.

But for the children, to whom six months can be a whole new life, the river would be remembered in other ways.

"Good-by, Mother," Nina Bernson said.

Her mother looked up.

"Come and give me a kiss."

Nina stood for a minute with her arm around her mother's neck, looking down at the half-typed page.

"What chapter are you on?"

"Next to last, thank God. It has to be in by the fifteenth." The thought of the deadline caused Nina's mother to release her abruptly, anxious to return to the race. "*Then* we'll get the rest of the advance, and we can use it! You've outgrown everything you own."

"I know."

"Well . . . run along now. You've got your lunch?"

"Yes."

"Your bathing suit?"

"Yes."

"Did you go to the—"

"Oh, Mother! Of course."

"All right. Run along."

The packed rhythm of the typewriter began again and Nina closed the door behind her. Her mother typed on for a line or two, stopped, pulled out the sheet and put another in and wrote a note to Kenneth, the man she would marry when the decree was final. . . . "Nina is so free here, so independent. For her the place is just a wonderful playground. . . ."

Broad brilliant light filled the morning. The air smelled strong, interesting: a sharp odor of sagebrush, river water, and baked rock, a Western smell. The leaves of the cottonwoods glittered like new dimes and quarters, and overhead the sky was powerful, cloudless, and burning with light. Swallows skipped on the air and Nina skipped along the river road where great thirsty trees, willows and cottonwoods, leaned toward the water, soaking their roots.

It was going to be terribly hot, every day was terribly hot now, and she was glad. There was cold sarsaparilla in her thermos bottle, and she and Frank and Eugenia would stay in the river all day. For the last two weeks they had lived in the river like otters.

After four months the road to town was as familiar to her as the park had been at home. Every day, at least twice, she walked this road, passing the orphanage with its big yard where she had never seen an orphan, and the Odd Fellows' hall where she had never seen an odd fellow, and the Italian people's chicken run, and the greenhouse full of begonias, and the glowering little khaki-colored cottage with the cross fox terrier and the big sign saying "Spiritual Readings." Every day she walked to one side or the other of the tree that grew in the middle of the path, murmuring "bread and butter," though she was all alone.

Before she saw it she could hear the waterfall, a heavy purring, pouring sound on this hot day. It was a man-made waterfall rushing sleekly over a dam and across a broad mossy platform before it dropped a second time. From it rose a churned-up fresh-water smell. Later she and Frank and Eugenia would play there; they would skid and scream on the slippery platform, or sit under the falling cascade wearing a heavy halter of cold water on their shoulders.

It was nearly noon, very hot. On the river's little islands, though the air was still, the thick gray willow foliage seemed to move and shift like the fur on Maltese cats. Men, a few, were fishing on the banks, and Indian women in faded calico were breaking off young willow wattles for their baskets. On the grass their babies lay in wicker chrysalids, staring at the naked sky. The cruel sun struck sparks from their little eyes and running noses; it took the color out of everything. Even the distant mountains looked like heaps of sand.

Far ahead of her Nina could see Frank and Eugenia running to meet her. Already she could hear the things rattling in their picnic baskets. Eugenia's straight blonde hair and Frank's tall pompadour flapped in the bright light. Eugenia was wearing one of her beautiful dresses, pink this time, and made of linen so stiff that after she had sat in it a while it would remain pressed up in an arc behind, showing the scalloped edges of her embroidered pants.

"Where *were* you? We've been waiting all *day*!" cried Eugenia imperiously. She was rather an imperious child. She and Frank lived in the hotel with their mother, a large golden woman who was always speaking to them in French or German, caressing them voluptuously, and laughing tenderly at their remarks with an opera singer's sumptuous laugh. They were all a little fat, and there was an air of plenty about them, an expansive sense of ease and extravagance and good will. The clothes they had! And new ones all the time. When Nina thought of her own mother pounding for funds at the typewriter, cursing at bills, and letting down hems, she felt a pang of anger, not at Eugenia's mother, alas, but at her own.

"Hurry, hurry!" cried Eugenia, sweeping her up in a gale of haste. "We're hot, we're roasticating, we're sweating. We've been waiting all day!"

They crossed the little red bridge to their special island, undressed in the bushes and put on their bathing suits. They hid their clothes and the lunch baskets under the giant dock leaves near the bank and ran carefully on their bare feet to the small collar of beach from which their swimming always started. The fringed willow saplings overhung it, they were everywhere, the air smelled of them and of the brown river water. Nina would never forget this smell: rank, willowy, weedy, rather dirty. But cool! A promise of coolness and wetness, of peace and play, with never a voice to warn against peril, nor any clock to consider but the sun in the sky.

                    "Last one in
                    Is a barrel of gin."

Eugenia sang it, but Nina beat her, she had longer

legs. The water was shallow, just up to the knees, but it was water at least, and she flung herself into it gladly, coming up dripping, with her braids full of algae, just in time to see Eugenia go belly-whopper in a huge ruff of raised water. She sank her body to the stream bed, idling along on her knees, with just her eyes and nose above the surface, and bubbles frilling out of her mouth. Frank lay down on the water and joined them slowly, dead man's float. They all did dead man's float, and then Nina and Eugenia had endurance contests under water, grunting and striving through the yellow currents. The water was warmed through, like broth, with here and there a wandering artery of cold. The bottom was soft as velvet, smoking upward when touched with toes or fingers.

"Genia!" called Frank.

"Yes?"

"Don't stay down too long."

"He's still a little scared," Eugenia murmured to Nina. Nina knew it. Frank had not known how to swim for very long. They were always pulling him out as he gurgled desperately for help. Yet fear never held him back; tense, with a band of blue around his mouth, he tried everything. He flung himself upon his fear, embraced it, as though his ardor could transform it into courage, as indeed it often had. Nina liked Frank. He was the first younger brother she had ever liked. He minded his own business. Yes, and he had dignity. At nine years old it could be said that he had dignity.

Though the river and the air were warm Nina was cold now. She walked to the shore trying not to shiver, hating her pale blue knees and ignominious goose flesh. Frank and Eugenia were luxuriously made, rounded and sleek, they never got cold, but Nina was thin as a bundle of twigs, with long straight braids, and sprinkled all over with freckles like cinnamon grains.

She brought the baskets from under the dock leaves and sat down on the shore. The dry air warmed her and she stopped shivering and after a while the others came out of the water and joined her. Heat, silence, and great blazing light poured down from heaven. The children were quiet, having shouted all the noise out of themselves for a while. They ate steadily, hardly speaking, watching their rejected crusts and lettuce leaves floating away on the stream's calm moving surface. Though the city was near at hand it seemed far distant. Drowned grass wagged to and fro in the current, and a little way from shore a grounded branch thrust upward from the water like an imploring arm. Rags of dried water moss stuck out from it in horizontal deer-slayer fringes, pointing the current.

"This is the best thing about this place," Nina said. "Playing in this river is the best. Before that the best thing was when I found the mariposa lilies. I went up there one day—you know, way outside town, where it's all sand

and sagebrush—and there they were, millions of them. Gosh, *millions* of them!"

But how could she tell them what it was like? Before she had known them she had spent many hours in those sun-dazzled wastes where at first there was nothing but rocks and sage and heaps of discarded trash: tiny sun-wizened leather shoes and tin cans rusted to lace. She had been contented, wandering, singing to herself, filling her pockets with red and purple stones, trying to hypnotize lizards, and searching for Indian relics which she never found. But soon the flowers began, all new ones that she had never seen before, and she brought them home in armloads, looking them up in the *Western Flower Book* until she knew them all; they were beginning to be an old story. And then one day, overnight it seemed, the mariposas had risen from the ground and opened their royal cups, and stood there waiting for her, rarely beautiful. Each grew a little apart from the others, a princess with a three-petaled crown. . . .

"I thought the best thing before this was the time we went down the mine," Frank said. "Or maybe when we killed the rattlesnake at the picnic."

"As far as I'm concerned the best thing was seeing Nazimova in *Salome*," Eugenia said, turning her gold bracelet with the tooth marks in it. "I saw it four times and some day I'll see it again."

They lay there for a while, idle, until the black flies

found them and then they went in the water again, traveling downstream. The shallow current carried them at a
gentle pace, the benevolent land slid by them, the benevolent bridges crept over their heads, and far away the
mountains were no longer like sand piles, but more like
heaped blue veils.

They lay on their backs as they passed Belle Isle where
the picnic benches and barbecue rings were. On Sunday
afternoons the place was an anthill. Fat ladies with babies
and pocketbooks and shade hats sat at the rough-hewn
tables chatting across the litter of bottles and paper cups.
Their men, in suspenders, lay dead on the grass with
newspaper pup tents over their faces, or fished with their
sons at the water's edge. Here and there, more or less
secluded from the others, young men and girls sat together
kissing. Nothing was concealed from the children, however, as they drifted by in the slow current staring, contented and curious. But today, a week day, there were
not many people, a fisherman or two, some girls with
a camera, a group of old men on a bench.

At the next island they came out of the water and
crossed to the other side where the rapids were. In this
narrow channel the river was brawling and tempestuous:
Nina and Eugenia flung themselves in with joyful screams,
letting the coffee-colored torrents hurl and buffet them
downstream, banging their bottoms over the rocks. Behind them came Frank, strained, enduring his fear pa-

tiently, smiling a set smile. They did this over and over again, toiling back along the island shore each time. When they were weary and waterlogged they let themselves drift to the still waters at the end of the rapids where big brown muffs of foam were standing, and dragged themselves out to rest on an unfamiliar bank among leaves and tall grass. Dragonflies were pinned motionless on the air, and great wailing mosquitoes came up out of the shadows to meet them.

"What do they live on between people?" Frank said.

Nina had often wondered this; she looked after him with respect as he wandered away.

"When are you leaving here?" she asked Eugenia.

"About the tenth of August, when Mama gets her decree."

"And you'll leave right away?"

"Oh, sure. Nothing to stay for, Mama says."

"I'll miss you."

"We'll write all the time. We'll always be best friends. When's yours getting her decree?"

"September, I guess."

"What's she getting it on?"

"What do you mean, getting it on?"

"The divorce. You know. Is it mental cruelty or incompatibility or nonsupport, or what?"

"Oh. Mental cruelty."

"Ours is for incompatibility."

The water slipped and rustled against the bank. "But

I never thought he was cruel," Nina said.

"I don't even know what incompatibility means, just exactly," Eugenia admitted. "Is yours going to get married again?"

"Yes, to a man named Kenneth, with a mustache. Is yours?"

"Ours both are."

"*Both*? How awful!"

"But you can't say it's for that when you get a divorce. You have to say it's mental cruelty or incompatibility or something, when really it's the other."

"I guess mine honestly didn't get along very well," Nina said loyally.

"Sometimes I hate them," Eugenia said. "Sometimes I just *hate* them."

Nina was silent. She slapped viciously at a mosquito and looked with satisfaction at the thready corpse on her arm and her own blood returned to her.

Frank came out of the bushes suddenly, with a yellowed willow leaf caught in his pompadour. "Hey, come here," he whispered, snickering. "I want to show you something, only shut up, don't make a sound."

They crawled after him through the willow thicket, stooped, breathless, giggling. It was hot and stuffy in there, and little half-transparent gnats flickered and hung about their eyes and ears, their tiny noise as thin and sticky as cobwebs.

Frank turned toward Nina and his sister. "Shut up,"

said his moving, silent lips. He got down on his hands and knees and crawled through the grass and they followed him. Then he stopped and pointed his finger at the screen of leaves through which he was peeping.

There in the sun-speckled grass two people lay, a man and a girl, mouth to mouth, body to body, devoured and devouring. The girl's black hair streamed in the grass like ink, her eyes were closed and so were the man's and his hand roved over her, loving her. Nina felt queer watching them, jealous and afraid. "Come away," she whispered, tugging at Eugenia's wrist. "Come away." Frank didn't want to come, he stayed where he was, watching, but she and Eugenia stole off through the sapling thicket, hot and silent.

"It was scary, kind of," Nina said, at last.

"I don't think so. I can't wait to get big," Eugenia said.

They had reached the river and were wading along the edge, which was brown, and shimmering with mica flakes, and warm as tears. Nina thought now of a day two weeks ago when Frank had stayed home with an earache and she and Eugenia had gone swimming by themselves. They had gone down the river, miles down, farther than they had ever been before, and when they climbed up the bushy bank they had found a man there, barring their way. He was a tall man with light bleached eyes and tan clothes. His hat was tan, too, and when he smiled at them, a slow, lingering smile, they saw that his teeth were tan as well.

"Hello, little girls."

He had some kind of accent, and his voice was lazy and gentle.

"Hello," they said.

"Where are you going, you two little girls?"

"Oh, no place, just exploring."

"Stay with me a little while, don't go. I like little girls. Stay and I will tell you a story."

What a strange man. They hesitated, smiling politely.

"But first you must kiss me," he said, coming close, and the little breeze that shuddered among the willow leaves at that moment seemed the first chill breath of danger. He had an arm around each of them, stroking Nina's long braid and holding Eugenia's plump shoulder.

Eugenia spoke first: "You let us go!"

"No, no, why will you go?" said the man, holding onto her. "Stay with me and I will take you to the carnival tonight. I will buy toys for you, Kewpie dolls, candy, many pretty things."

"You let us go!" shouted Eugenia, pulling away.

"Thanks just the same," quavered Nina, jerking her braid out of his hand, and they began to run. It was terrible; the man came after them. They could hear him stumbling and crashing and yelling swear words at them, and it was worse than any nightmare except that they were free to run—not rooted helpless to the spot—and finally he got tired and stopped chasing them, but they kept on running anyway until they came to one of the bridges, and they never went back to that place again. They never said anything about it at home, either, even to Frank. Nina felt sick at her stomach whenever she thought about it, and she thought about it now.

"Those two people. They were like the man in tan that time."

Eugenia turned around and looked at her.

"They were nothing like that."

They splashed on in silence. The afternoon was hot and still, the noise of the rapids a whisper in the distance.

"Let's go to the falls," said Eugenia after a while.

"Let's!" cried Nina, eager and relieved.

Beneath the second fall there was a wide deep pool, faintly agitated always from the plunging waters that fed it. This was the only possible diving place in that part of the river and somebody had built a plank spring-board out from the platform. Sometimes the pool was taken over by a gang of big croaking adolescent boys and then Nina and Eugenia kept to the outskirts prudently, but today they had the place to themselves.

Repeatedly they dived into the dark blue-brown pool, their legs spraddled out and their stomachs stinging. Frank appeared from nowhere and joined them, but he would not dive. He stepped down from one bank and swam dutifully and effortfully to the opposite one where he rested, gathering courage for the return journey across the gleaming menacing surface beneath which death or ignominy waited.

Having dived, drowned, ducked, until they had drunkard's eyes and inflamed nostrils, the girls went up to the platform to sing and dance, for the place reminded them of a stage. It was tricky and dangerous there, they slipped and fell repeatedly, each sick with laughter at the mishaps of the other, and both smeared all over with oily streaks of water moss. They capered and shrieked and fell, and beyond and below them, Frank plied to and fro across the pool, joyless and undeviating as a ferryboat. Now and then he called to them and they replied, but a time came, halfway across, when his call was lost in the noise they were making above the noise of the water. He called a second time but still they did not hear him and he began to feel panic. His voice cheeped out like a bird's, he lost his balance in the water, a wave flew into his mouth, he choked, and the death and ignominy at the dark pool's bottom swam up lazily to find him. Infinitely far away on the shore the sweet trees bowed and shook their leaves to him, the sunshine and warm air of life continued and would continue without him. . . . One more cry, one more . . .

Nina and Eugenia saw him at the same moment. They saw his terrified eyes, his sick face; they saw but did not hear the last cry for help: it came out in a bubble as he went down in the dark water. Time stopped. It held still in a great suspended sensation of anguish as they dived. The water was opaque; they struggled in a bland secretive element that showed them nothing. Up they came purple-faced, gasping; down they went again, with their eyes staring against dimness and their hearts ringing like bells in their chests. Eugenia got hold of him first and came up screaming for Nina. Together they pulled him, inert, terrifying, a stranger, to the bank. "He's dead, he's dead," Eugenia kept sobbing. "Oh, what will Mama say?" But when they got him there, and he fell from their hands face down on the sand, the water came out of his nose and mouth in a gush, his eyes opened once and closed immediately as he began to cry. He strangled and retched and wept as Eugenia pounded his back.

"Anyway you're alive, Frankie," she said, very loud, as though he must hear her from a distance. "You're alive, we saved your life."

"You're going to be all right, Frankie," Nina assured him stroking his wet upstanding pompadour with her wet palm. "Everything's all right now." She was crying, too, they all were, from terror and exultation and relief.

Frank sat up after a while, still with that transfixed, affronted look on his face. His teeth were chattering, and they put their arms around him, having nothing else to warm him with.

"Don't tell Mama," he said, weakly.

"Do we ever tell?" said Eugenia. "We know better."

"Cross our hearts," said Nina. She had a feeling of adequacy and grace; it was wonderful how children were always sparing their parents. They had already spared their parents every account of Frank's frequent rescues from drowning; they had spared them the news of the man in tan, and of the time they discovered that they had been playing at the mouth of a sewer, and of several other events which could only have worried them needlessly.

Frank gave a long trembling sigh, and his shivering abated; but they continued to sit there linked together, weary and contented. A pinkish light had come into the afternoon, and though the sun was far from setting there was an evening feeling in the air. The swallows knew it and left their low skimming to soar aloft in garrulous crowds.

"Maybe it's time to go home."

"I suppose . . ."

But for a few more minutes they stayed as they were, reluctant to start the long trip back, all against the current, to the island where their clothes were hidden. It always took a good half-hour, partly because of the current, partly because of all the swimming that must be done on the way, and all the shores that must be visited. When they were dressed they were tired, subdued, half washed away. The river had taken as much as it had given.

"Good-by, Eugenia, good-by, Frank."

"Good-by, Neen."

"See you tomorrow?"

"Oh sure, we'll 'phone you."

"Well, good-by."

"Good-by."

"Good-by."

The sun was almost on a level with Nina now, and facing her. Its late shine put golden edges on the leaves, gilded the river. The day was over. Someone stood on every lawn holding a hose; the soft sifting noise was everywhere, and overhead the cottonwood trees picked it up with a lofty simmering rustle as the wind stirred. Every car was home in its garage, every father was back from work, and all the children back from play. The air smelled of food. The Italian people were eating their supper under the grape trellis, quacking and cackling at a great rate and sending up a fume of garlic to strengthen the evening air.

The families were together again, called by the hour to their common roof. Once more they had each other, for better or worse, to joke and eat and quarrel with. Frank and Eugenia, two together, had the big benevolent beauty who was their mother to welcome them home. She, Nina, had her own mother. But in the fall her mother would have Kenneth, too. . . .

The mountains that ringed the world were purple

now, and old and cold: careless and distant as the Great Wall of China. Under her wishbone a pain began, but she hated the pain, she had had it before, and would not stand for it. She began to skip along the path singing "Water Boy" to distract herself and any tree or blade of grass that might be watching, and just then Mr. Reemer, their neighbor, came along in his windy old Chandler and gave her a lift home, so everything was better.

It looked as though her mother had not moved all day. Though the room was shadowed she sat at the typewriter, still, the goose-neck lamp making a lake of light around her.

"Home at last!" she said to Nina, leaning back in the chair and stretching her tired arms over her head. "Another day gone. Oh, will the time ever be over?" she cried. "Six months is a long, long sentence, isn't it?"

Nina put the end of her wet braid into her mouth and chewed on it. It tasted of rank river water. Let the time never end, she thought, watching her mother. Let the lawyer tell her she'll have to stay a whole year. Two whole years.

Her mother sighed and turned in her chair, smiling at her.

"Did you have fun, darling? What did you do?"

"Oh, nothing," Nina said slowly, through her braid. "Swam. Played. Nothing much."

TOMORROW AND TOMORROW AND SO FORTH
John Updike

Whirling, talking, 11D began to enter Room 109. From the quality of their excitement Mark Prosser guessed it would rain. He had been teaching high school for three years, yet his students still impressed him; they were such sensitive animals. They reacted so infallibly to merely barometric pressure.

In the doorway, Brute Young paused while little Barry Snyder giggled at his elbow. Barry's stagy laugh rose and fell, dipping down toward some vile secret that had to be tasted and retasted, then soaring artificially to proclaim that he, little Barry, shared such a secret with the school's fullback. Being Brute's stooge was precious to Barry. The fullback paid no attention to him; he twisted his neck to stare at something not yet coming through the door. He yielded heavily to the procession pressing him forward.

Right under Prosser's eyes, like a murder suddenly appearing in an annalistic frieze of kings and queens, someone stabbed a girl in the back with a pencil. She ignored the assault saucily. Another hand yanked out Geoffrey Langer's shirt-tail. Geoffrey, a bright student, was uncertain whether to laugh it off or defend himself with anger, and made a weak, half-turning gesture of compromise, wearing an expression of distant arrogance that Prosser instantly coordinated with feelings of fear he used to have. All along the line, in the glitter of key chains and the acute angles of turned-back shirt cuffs, an electricity was expressed which simple weather couldn't generate.

Mark wondered if today Gloria Angstrom wore that sweater, an ember-pink angora, with very brief sleeves. The virtual sleevelessness was the disturbing factor: the exposure of those two serene arms to the air, white as thighs against the delicate wool.

His guess was correct. A vivid pink patch flashed through the jiggle of arms and shoulders as the final knot of youngsters entered the room.

"Take your seats," Mr. Prosser said. "Come on. Let's go."

Most obeyed, but Peter Forrester, who had been at the center of the group around Gloria, still lingered in the doorway with her, finishing some story, apparently determined to make her laugh or gasp. When she did gasp, he tossed his head with satisfaction. His orange hair bobbed. Redheads are all alike, Mark thought, with their white eyelashes and pale puffy faces and thyroid eyes, their mouths always twisted with preposterous self-confidence. Bluffers, the whole bunch.

When Gloria, moving in a considered, stately way, had taken her seat, and Peter had swerved into his, Mr. Prosser said, "Peter Forrester."

"Yes?" Peter rose, scrabbling through his book for the right place.

"Kindly tell the class the exact meaning of the words 'Tomorrow, and tomorrow, and tomorrow/Creeps in this petty pace from day to day.'"

Peter glanced down at the high-school edition of *Macbeth* lying open on his desk. One of the duller girls tittered expectantly from the back of the room. Peter was popular with the girls; girls that age had minds like moths.

"Peter. With your book shut. We have all memorized this passage for today. Remember?" The girl in the back of the room squealed in delight. Gloria laid her own book face-open on her desk, where Peter could see it.

Peter shut his book with a bang and stared into Gloria's. "Why," he said at last, "I think it means pretty much what it says."

"Which is?"

"Why, that tomorrow is something we often think about. It creeps into our conversation all the time. We couldn't make any plans without thinking about tomorrow."

"I see. Then you would say that Macbeth is here

refering to the, the date-book aspect of life?"

Geoffrey Langer laughed, no doubt to please Mr. Prosser. For a moment, he *was* pleased. Then he realized he had been playing for laughs at a student's expense.

His paraphrase had made Peter's reading of the lines seem more ridiculous than it was. He began to retract. "I admit—"

But Peter was going on; redheads never know when to quit. "Macbeth means that if we quit worrying about tomorrow, and just lived for today, we could appreciate all the wonderful things that are going on under our noses."

Mark considered this a moment before he spoke. He would not be sarcastic. "Uh, without denying that there is truth in what you say, Peter, do you think it likely that Macbeth, in his situation, would be expressing such"—he couldn't help himself—"such sunny sentiments?"

Geoffrey laughed again. Peter's neck reddened; he studied the floor. Gloria glared at Mr. Prosser, the anger in her face clearly meant for him to see.

Mark hurried to undo his mistake. "Don't misunderstand me, please," he told Peter. "I don't have all the answers myself. But it seems to me the whole speech, down to 'Signifying nothing,' is saying that life is—well, a *fraud*. Nothing wonderful about it."

"Did Shakespeare really think that?" Geoffrey Langer asked, a nervous quickness pitching his voice high.

Mark read into Geoffrey's question his own adolescent

premonitions of the terrible truth. The attempt he must make was plain. He told Peter he could sit down and looked through the window toward the steadying sky. The clouds were gaining intensity. "There is," Mr. Prosser slowly began, "much darkness in Shakespeare's work, and no play is darker than *Macbeth*. The atmosphere is poisonous, oppressive. One critic has said that in this play, humanity suffocates." This was too fancy.

"In the middle of his career, Shakespeare wrote plays about men like Hamlet and Othello and Macbeth—men who aren't allowed by their society, or bad luck, or some minor flaw in themselves, to become the great men they might have been. Even Shakespeare's comedies of this period deal with a world gone sour. It is as if he had seen through the bright, bold surface of his earlier comedies and histories and had looked upon something terrible. It frightened him, just as some day it may frighten some of you." In his determination to find the right words, he had been staring at Gloria, without meaning to. Embarrassed, she nodded, and, realizing what had happened, he smiled at her.

He tried to make his remarks gentler, even diffident. "But then I think Shakespeare sensed a redeeming truth. His last plays are serene and symbolical, as if he had pierced through the ugly facts and reached a realm where the facts are again beautiful. In this way, Shakespeare's total work is a more complete image of life than that of any other writer, except perhaps for Dante, an Italian poet who wrote several centuries earlier." He had been taken far from the Macbeth soliloquy. Other teachers had been happy to tell him how the kids made a game of getting him talking. He looked toward Geoffrey. The boy was doodling on his tablet, indifferent. Mr. Prosser concluded, "The last play Shakespeare wrote is an extra-ordinary poem called *The Tempest*. Some of you may want to read it for your next book reports—the ones due May 10th. It's a short play."

The class had been taking a holiday. Barry Snyder was snicking BBs off the blackboard and glancing over at Brute Young to see if he noticed. "Once more, Barry," Mr. Prosser said, "and out you go." Barry blushed, and grinned to cover the blush, his eyeballs sliding toward Brute. The dull girl in the rear of the room was putting on lipstick. "Put that away, Alice," Mr. Prosser commanded. She giggled and obeyed. Sejak, the Polish boy who worked nights, was asleep at his desk, his cheek white with pressure against the varnished wood, his mouth sagging side-wise. Mr. Prosser had an impulse to let him sleep. But the impulse might not be true kindness, but just the self-congratulatory, kindly pose in which he sometimes discovered himself. Besides, one breach of discipline encouraged others. He strode down the aisle and shook Sejak awake. Then he turned his attention to the mumble growing at the front of the room.

Peter Forrester was whispering to Gloria, trying to make her laugh. The girl's face, though, was cool and solemn, as if a thought had been provoked in her head. Perhaps at least *she* had been listening to what Mr. Prosser had been saying. With a bracing sense of chivalrous intercession, Mark said, "Peter. I gather from this noise that you have something to add to your theories."

Peter responded courteously. "No, sir. I honestly don't understand the speech. Please, sir, what *does* it mean?"

This candid admission and odd request stunned the class. Every white, round face, eager, for once, to learn, turned toward Mark. He said, "I don't know. I was hoping *you* would tell *me*."

In college, when a professor made such a remark, it was with grand effect. The professor's humility, the necessity for creative interplay between teacher and student were dramatically impressed upon the group. But to 11D, ignorance in an instructor was as wrong as a hole in a roof. It was as if he had held forty strings pulling forty faces taut toward him and then had slashed the strings. Heads waggled, eyes dropped, voices buzzed. Some of the discipline problems, like Peter Forrester, smirked signals to one another.

"Quiet!" Mr. Prosser shouted. "All of you. Poetry isn't arithmetic. There's no single right answer. I don't want to force my impression on you, even if I *have* had much more experience with literature." He made this last clause very loud and distinct, and some of the weaker students seemed reassured. "I know none of *you* want that," he told them.

Whether or not they believed him, they subsided, somewhat. Mark judged he could safely reassume his human-among-humans attitude again. He perched on the edge of the desk and leaned forward beseechingly. "Now, honestly. Don't any of you have some personal feelings about the lines that you would like to share with the class and me?"

One hand, with a flowered handkerchief balled in it, unsteadily rose. "Go ahead, Teresa," Mr. Prosser said encouragingly. She was a timid, clumsy girl whose mother was a Jehovah's Witness.

"It makes me think of cloud shadows," Teresa said.

Geoffrey Langer laughed. "Don't be rude, Geoff," Mr. Prosser said sideways, softly, before throwing his voice forward: "Thank you, Teresa. I think that's an interesting and valid impression. Cloud movement has something in it of the slow, monotonous rhythm one feels in the line 'Tomorrow, and tomorrow, and tomorrow.' It's a very gray line, isn't it, class?" No one agreed or disagreed.

Beyond the windows actual clouds were bunching rapidly, and erratic sections of sunlight slid around the room. Gloria's arm, crooked gracefully above her head, turned gold. "Gloria?" Mr. Prosser asked.

She looked up from something on her desk with a face

of sullen radiance. "I think what Teresa said was very good," she said, glaring in the direction of Geoffrey Langer. Geoffrey chuckled defiantly. "And I have a question. What does 'petty pace' mean?"

"It means the trivial day-to-day sort of life that, say, a bookkeeper or a bank clerk leads. Or a schoolteacher," he added, smiling.

She did not smile back. Thought wrinkles irritated her perfect brow. "But Macbeth has been fighting wars, and killing kings, and being a king himself, and all," she pointed out.

"Yes, but it's just these acts Macbeth is condemning as 'nothing.' Can you see that?"

Gloria shook her head. "Another thing I worry about —isn't it silly for Macbeth to be talking to himself right in the middle of this war, with his wife just dead, and all?"

"I don't think so, Gloria. No matter how fast events happen, thought is faster."

His answer was weak; everyone knew it, even if Gloria hadn't mused, supposedly to herself, but in a voice the entire class could hear, "It seems so *stupid*."

Mark winced, pierced by the awful clarity with which his students saw him. Through their eyes, how queer he looked, with his long hands, and his horn-rimmed glasses, and his hair never slicked down, all wrapped up in "literature," where, when things get rough, the king mumbles a poem nobody understands. The delight Mr. Prosser took in such crazy junk made not only his good sense but his masculinity a matter of doubt. It was gentle of them not to laugh him out of the room. He looked down and rubbed his fingertips together, trying to erase the chalk dust. The class noise sifted into unnatural quiet. "It's getting late," he said finally. "Let's start the recitations of the memorized passage. Bernard Amilson, you begin."

Bernard had trouble enunciating, and his rendition began " 'T'mau 'n' t'mau 'n' t'mau.' " It was reassuring, the extent to which the class tried to repress its laughter. Mr. Prosser wrote "A" in his marking book opposite Bernard's name. He always gave Bernard A on recitations, despite the school nurse, who claimed there was nothing organically wrong with the boy's mouth.

It was the custom, cruel but traditional, to deliver recitations from the front of the room. Alice, when her turn came, was reduced to a helpless state by the first funny face Peter Forrester made at her. Mark let her hang up there a good minute while her face ripened to cherry redness, and at last forgave her. She may try it later. Many of the youngsters knew the passage gratifyingly well, though there was a tendency to leave out the line "To the last syllable of recorded time" and to turn "struts and frets" into "frets and struts" or simply "struts and struts." Even Sejak, who couldn't have looked at the passage before he came to class, got through it as far as "And then is heard no more."

Geoffrey Langer showed off, as he always did, by interrupting his own recitation with bright questions. " 'Tomorrow, and tomorrow, and tomorrow,' " he said, " 'creeps in'—shouldn't that be '*creep* in,' Mr. Prosser?"

"It is 'creep*s*.' The trio is in effect singular. Go on." Mr. Prosser was tired of coddling Langer. If you let them, these smart students will run away with the class. "Without the footnotes."

" 'Creep*sss* in this petty pace from day to day, to the last syllable of recorded time, and all our yesterdays have lighted fools the way to dusty death. Out, out—' "

"No, no!" Mr. Prosser jumped out of his chair. "This is poetry. Don't mushmouth it! Pause a little after 'fools.' " Geoffrey looked genuinely startled this time, and Mark himself did not quite understand his annoyance and, mentally turning to see what was behind him, seemed to glimpse in the humid undergrowth the two stern eyes of the indignant look Gloria had thrown Geoffrey. He glimpsed himself in the absurd position of acting as Gloria's champion in her private war with this intelligent boy. He sighed apologetically. "Poetry is made up of lines," he began, turning to the class. Gloria was passing a note to Peter Forrester.

The rudeness of it! To pass notes during a scolding that she herself had caused! Mark caged in his hand the girl's frail wrist and ripped the note from her fingers. He read it to himself, letting the class see he was reading it, though he despised such methods of discipline. The note went:

Pete—I think you're *wrong* about Mr. Prosser. I think he's wonderful and I get a lot out of his class. He's heavenly with poetry. I think I love him. I really do *love* him. So there.

Mr. Prosser folded the note once and slipped it into his side coat pocket. "See me after class, Gloria," he said. Then, to Geoffrey, "Let's try it again. Begin at the beginning."

While the boy was reciting the passage, the buzzer sounded the end of the period. It was the last class of the day. The room quickly emptied, except for Gloria. The noise of lockers slamming open and books being thrown against metal and shouts drifted in.

"Who has a car?"

"Lend me a cig, pig."

"We can't have practice in this slop."

Mark hadn't noticed exactly when the rain started, but it was coming down fast now. He moved around the room with the window pole, closing windows and pulling down shades. Spray bounced in on his hands. He began to talk to Gloria in a crisp voice that, like his device of shutting the windows, was intended to protect them both from embarrassment.

"About note passing." She sat motionless at her desk in the front of the room, her short, brushed-up hair like a cool torch. From the way she sat, her naked arms folded at her breasts and her shoulders hunched, he felt she was chilly. "It is not only rude to scribble when a teacher is talking, it is stupid to put one's words down on paper, where they look much more foolish than they might have sounded if spoken." He leaned the window pole in its corner and walked toward his desk.

"And about love. 'Love' is one of those words that illustrate what happens to an old, overworked language. These days, with movie stars and crooners and preachers and psychiatrists all pronouncing the word, it's come to mean nothing but a vague fondness for something. In this sense, I love the rain, this blackboard, these desks, you. It means nothing, you see, whereas once the word signified a quite explicit thing—a desire to share all you own and are with someone else. It is time we coined a new word to mean that, and when you think up the word *you* want to use, I suggest that you be economical with it. Treat it as something you can spend only once—if not for your own sake, for the good of the language." He walked over to his own desk and dropped two pencils on it, as if to say, "That's all."

"I'm sorry," Gloria said.

Rather surprised, Mr. Prosser said, "Don't be."

"But you don't understand."

"Of course I don't. I probably never did. At your age, I was like Geoffrey Langer."

"I bet you weren't." The girl was almost crying; he was sure of that.

"Come on, Gloria. Run along. Forget it." She slowly cradled her books between her bare arm and her sweater, and left the room with that melancholy shuffling teen-age gait, so that her body above her thighs seemed to float over the desks.

What was it, Mark asked himself, these kids were after? What did they want? Glide, he decided, the quality of glide. To slip along, always in rhythm, always cool, the little wheels humming under you, going nowhere special. If Heaven existed, that's the way it would be there. "He's heavenly with poetry." They loved the word. Heaven was in half their songs.

"Christ, he's humming," Strunk, the physical ed teacher, had come into the room without Mark's noticing. Gloria had left the door ajar.

"Ah," Mark said, "a fallen angel, full of grit."

"What the hell makes you so happy?"

"I'm not happy, I'm just serene. I don't know why you don't appreciate me."

"Say." Strunk came up an aisle with a disagreeably effeminate waddle, pregnant with gossip. "Did you hear about Murchison?"

"No." Mark mimicked Strunk's whisper.

"He got the pants kidded off him today."

"Oh dear."

Strunk started to laugh, as he always did before beginning a story. "You know what a goddam lady's man he thinks he is?"

"You bet," Mark said, although Strunk said that about every male member of the faculty.

"You have Gloria Angstrom, don't you?"

"You bet."

"Well, this morning Murky intercepts a note she was writing, and the note says what a damn neat guy she thinks Murchison is and how she *loves* him!" Strunk waited for Mark to say something, and then, when he didn't, continued, "You could see he was tickled pink. But —get this—it turns out at lunch that the same damn thing happened to Freyburg in history yesterday!" Strunk laughed and cracked his knuckles viciously. "The girl's too dumb to have thought it up herself. We all think it was Peter Forrester's idea."

"Probably was," Mark agreed. Strunk followed him out to his locker, describing Murchison's expression when Freyburg (in all innocence, mind you) told what had happened to him.

Mark turned the combination of his locker, 18–24–3. "Would you excuse me, Dave?" he said. "My wife's in town waiting."

Strunk was too thick to catch Mark's anger. "I got to get over to the gym. Can't take the little darlings outside in the rain; their mommies'll write notes to teacher." He clattered down the hall and wheeled at the far end, shouting, "Now don't tell You-know-who!"

Mr. Prosser took his coat from the locker and shrugged it on. He placed his hat upon his head. He fitted his rubbers over his shoes, pinching his fingers painfully, and lifted his umbrella off the hook. He thought of opening it right there in the vacant hall, as a kind of joke, and decided not to. The girl had been almost crying; he was sure of that.

THE SMALL PORTION
H. E. Bates

The girl and her mother had driven down from the mountains in August, by way of Cortina and the Vale de Cembra and the towns of Lombardy, at the time when the wild cyclamen were in bloom. It was still hot, with distances of smoky glass, when they reached the lakes in September.

"What dish is this? Do you speak English? What do you call it?"

Mrs. Carey poked with her knife at the main luncheon dish so that the flash of sun on steel made white winks on the underbellies of the terrace umbrellas.

"It is a sort of pasta, madame. A sort of—"

"A sort of what? What is this green material? Why is it green?"

"That is the pasta itself, madame. Pasta Verdi. Green macaroni."

"It looks most extraordinary." Mrs. Carey poked at it again.

"It is very good, madame," the waiter said. "You will like it, I'm sure—"

"Give us both a very small portion." Mrs. Carey waved her knife again as if to sever the dish into even smaller segments than those the waiter was spooning. "Smaller— smaller—not so much as that. We do not like large portions. You understand? We don't eat much. We do not like large portions."

"Yes, madame."

"No cheese. No cheese. We do not like cheese."

With pale eyes the girl sat staring at the lake. The water was a strong blue-green, with distances of molten rose, and above it a sky of misty torrid blue in which the edges of the horizon were completely dissolved. Below the terrace a few people were still swimming; she saw a flash of brown arms on a diving board.

"The lake looks lovely—"

"Eat your food while it's hot. The lake is very deep," Mrs. Carey said. "It is fourteen hundred and fifty feet deep in one place. I was reading about it yesterday."

The face of the girl had the soft colorless plumpness of a big summer apple that has grown unexposed to sun. With unresistant eyes she stared at the lake, eating slowly. She had seen Cortina and Verona and Bellagio and Como and Ponte Tresa, or rather she had been shown them all; but she could not help feeling that Maggiore, now, was the most beautiful of them all.

"It would be nice to stay here—"

"Well, I don't know. We shall see. We shall see what this place is like." Mrs. Carey peered with spectacled intensity at something among the macaroni. "Those are pieces of spinach stalk. They've not been sieved properly. Put them on the side of your plate if you don't want them."

While her mother sat microscopically peering the girl looked up.

"Those people we saw at the Arena at Verona are here," she said. "Mr. and Mrs. Smithson and the boy. They're just coming on to the terrace—"

"Concentrate on your food. I don't know that we altogether—"

"Well, hullo!" Mr. Smithson said. "Small world!"

Mr. Smithson wore a bright blue linen shirt with a deep open neck that showed a forest of strong black chest hairs.

"You remember Mrs. Carey and Josephine, Mother," he said. "The amphitheater at Verona. Biggest in Italy or something, isn't it?"

"After the Colosseum," Mrs. Carey said.

"Well, how nice!" Mrs. Smithson said. "What a nice surprise! You remember our boy, don't you, Mrs. Carey? You remember John?"

The black hair of the young man was still wet from swimming. Mrs. Smithson, small, fair, sandy-eyed, was blistered in unhealthy crimson patches from too much sun.

"I'm afraid we're late for lunch," she said. "But we waited for John. He kept having another swim. The waiters don't like it here if you're late. One said 'One thirty, one thirty!' to me yesterday."

"It's my fault," the young man said. "I just had to go in again."

"Well, we must go," Mrs. Smithson said. "We want to get lunch over and go to Orta this afternoon."

"Ah! yes, the little lake."

"Oh! you know it?"

"Of course. It's well known."

"Well, why don't you come over with us?" Mrs. Smithson said and Mr. Smithson too said why didn't they come over?

"We're going to look over a house there," he said. "A villa or something. Just for fun. We saw the advert in a paper. Why don't you come over?"

"I rather like to rest after lunch."

"Well, why doesn't Josephine come over?" Mr. Smithson said and Mrs. Smithson too said why didn't Josephine come over?

"Would you find that amusing, dear?"

"I—well, if it's—"

"Yes!" Mr. Smithson said. "Of course. Why not? We've got the Bentley. We can have tea there. It'll be fun."

"Well, if you think you'd find it amusing, dear—"

"Good!" Mr. Smithson said. "That's the stuff. Good! We'll pick you up at two."

It was just after three o'clock, in the heat of the afternoon, when the young man drove the car into the little enclosed piazza, under a line of plane trees, on the edge of the lake.

"Did you have the green macaroni?" Mr. Smithson had said several times. "Something in it was salt. The cheese in it or something. God, it was salt—my tongue's hanging out."

"Ask the boatman if that's the island," Mrs. Smithson said. "I suppose we have to row over there."

The boy, by the side of the mottled leather-faced Italian boatman, looked very tall, his flanks smooth and slim in their fresh coppery linen trousers.

"Yes, that's it," he said. "*Isola san Giulio*. That's a monastery or something—"

"I think it's a Basilica," the girl said.

"Shall we have a cup o' tea first?" Mr. Smithson said. "God, my tongue's like emery paper."

"Oh! I don't know," Mrs. Smithson said. "Do we want to row over there? Just to see a house? We'd never live there, anyway. I tell you what—you go, John. You and Josephine. Dad and me'll sit here and have tea while you go. Eh, Dad?"

"Do what you like," Mr. Smithson said. "But I

149

got to have a wet of some sort—"

"All right, John and Josephine go and we'll wait for you." She smiled with bright, encouraging, sandy-eyed laughter. "John and Josephine—that sounds rather nice, doesn't it? They go well together. Wasn't there a book with that name?"

On the island, from a flight of steps under the Basilica, a street not wide enough for a car went winding up from the water's edge like a cool stone gully between high houses of crumbling stucco or under walls crested with dark spires of cypress and pink bushes of oleander. There was a sleepiness over everything, a drugged siesta silence that absorbed, as into thick wool, the sound of footsteps.

"Where could the house be?" the young man said. "Villa Agordo—that's a nice name, I think, don't you?"

"Yes."

"It's like a maze," he said. Walls of great height, joined across in places by little insecure bridges connecting the top storeys of villas with terraces of vine, kept out the sun. The tiny street curled round and round, deep-cut, trafficless, without people, with no footsteps but their own.

"We'll have to ask," he said, "if there's anybody to ask." His eyes were suddenly amused, impish, blackly twinkling. "Shall I shout? Do you think someone will answer if I yell 'Anyone at home?' "

"Oh! no." She could hear the profound silence of the

little street pressing down on her, almost singing, as she stood there.

"I'm going to chance it," he said. She watched his face lift, break into a broad smile and yell: "Anybody there? Anybody at home?"

It might have been that his voice set off a spring in the high walls, flicking open the windows of a bed-room.

"Signor?"

"Villa Agordo," he said. "Do you know the Villa Agordo?"

"At the top of the street. The white one."

"Thank you. Would there be someone there?"

"Look over the garden wall and shout 'Gina!'" she said. "Gina's there—she'll show you over."

As they walked up the street he said once or twice how queer it all was: how odd the atmosphere, wheel-less and quiet and sleepy, in the middle of the lake, in the heat of the afternoon. He said once that he thought it was like a deserted ship, moored and left to rot, and that you could almost smell the timbers, mouldering away in the water.

"I think it's beautiful," she said. "Away from every-thing."

"Or it might be the plague," he said. "And everyone driven out."

"It wasn't the plague," she said. "It was serpents. They

had to be driven out. It was a saint named St. Julius who drove them out."

"Oh! I say!" He was mocking her gently; but she was still not sure of it and she felt herself flushing. "Where did you find all *that* out?"

"I read it in the guide."

"Not mother?"

She knew then that he was mocking, and she hated her mother.

"Gina!" He called twice over a wall, through a deep garden, to where pergolas of vine made another maze down to the edge of a stony slipway, where two boats were moored.

"Oh! you want to look at the villa?"

"Yes, please."

She was an Italian woman of great pleasantness, soft-armed, amiable, with drowsy dignity, who took them into the tall old house where, as he whispered once to the girl, he thought no one had lived since St. Julius had driven out the toads.

"Not toads," she said. "Serpents."

"Well, serpents or toads," he said. "We don't always have to be so accurate, do we?"

As she took them from floor to floor, by one mouldering staircase and another, under draperies that were decaying piecemeal where they hung and past beds sagging and drunk with the weight of invisible sleepers in shuttered bedrooms, the woman occasionally bathed them both in her drowsy, amiable smile.

"For you?" she said. "The house?" She giggled. "There are plenty of rooms to fill—plenty for *bambini*—eh?"

"Well—I don't know. We might consider it—"

Lightly he mocked the woman and then with gravity looked down at the girl.

"Would you like to live here?"

"I'm not sure. I think so. Would you?"

He looked straight into her eyes and warmly and boldly through them.

"Might be nice," he said.

"Go out on the terrace," the woman said. "Bella vista —bella vista—it is very beautiful. The rooms are dark today because the shutters are up."

On the terrace a broken oleander, its flowers pitched face downwards on the stone, and a small torn banana tree, were all that remained of a lakeside garden that had clearly once been very beautiful.

"Would you really like to live here?"

She stood looking across the lake: villas like toy white blocks among distant cypresses and above them terraces of vine melting into mountains and above that mountains melting into sky.

"I think it would be heavenly. I should love it," she said.

For almost all the rest of the time, as they stood staring

over the hot tranquil lake, she did not know if he was mocking.

"Well, why not?" he said. "I'll talk to mother and mother will talk to Dad. Instead of a new Bentley next year he could buy the villa. That's what cotton does for you. If you think about it, there's no reason why not, is there?"

"I suppose not."

"Not even the serpents," he said. "*They've* been driven out—we wouldn't have *them* to bother us anyway."

All the way back, through the deep gully of the curving street, he kept up that half-teasing, half-serious fondness in his way of speaking. The woman Gina had stood for a long time lifting her hand in farewell, beaming on them her own fondness in cow-warm smiles, as if in amiable dedication to them as lovers.

"You know, I've just thought of something," he said. "The streets are the tracks the serpents made."

He stopped. They were in a narrow place, a twist in the street that left them isolated. Far above them the dome of the Basilica burned in the sky and from somewhere she could hear the sound of a fountain dribbling water.

A moment later he was pressing her against the wall. Over the wall a high oleander poured wasted pink blossoms, vanilla-soft, into dark shade. The island about her melted completely into the deep substance of this one half-sweet scent and as he kissed her she stared high above the Basilica, eyes wide open, with shocked wonder, at the sky.

Afterwards, as he laughed down at her, she had no way of knowing if the tenderness of it, the easy warmth, had separated itself finally from mocking. She felt there was a skein of rose-shadowy air in front of her face and she kept trying to wipe it away.

"You see," he said, "there's nothing to stop anything if you really want to."

When they had rowed back to the piazza on the mainland his mother said:

"Well, what was it like? Tell us."

"Marvelous," he said. "You've got to ask Dad to buy it. It has a banana plantation. Grapes, figs, two boats and a view to Monte Rosa. We could live on fish and fruit—live for nothing. Absolutely."

"Oh! hark at him!" Mrs. Smithson said. "When can you believe him? You really can't, can you? What was it really like?"

"Awful," he said. "God-awful. It hasn't been lived in since St. Julius threw out the toads. You should see the curtains."

"St. Julius who threw what?" Mrs. Smithson laughed with tears of doting in her eyes. "You must have had a good time out there. Did you," she said to the girl, "have a good time?"

"It was beautiful," the girl said.

"You'll have to be careful! You don't have to take too much notice! They tell him I spoil him!" she said.

The girl and her mother drove on after lunch the following day. Mr. Smithson, at the last moment, stood on the terrace with his camera pressed against the wiry hairs of his chest. "Smile!" he kept saying. "Smile! We must have a smile," and Mrs. Smithson stood with one arm about the waist of her son.

"Good-bye!" everyone shouted and Mr. Smithson, having taken the photograph, called:

"May see you in Pisa—leaning against the leaning tower!"

"We are going another way. We are going to Monte Rosa," Mrs. Carey said.

"Don't forget the serpents!" the young man called.

In the midafternoon the car wound slowly up into the mountains. With her round colorless unripened apple face the girl stared forward into the haze of sun and dust and high places. Once again peasant children were selling, on the roadsides, little bunches of chalk-rose cyclamen, wild from the hills.

Once or twice she stared back.

"What is it?" her mother said. "Don't fidget. What are you looking at? I hope you haven't forgotten anything again?"

"Only the lake," she said.

"Not like you did at Verona? You said 'No' that time

and we had to go back. You're sure you haven't forgotten anything?"

"No," the girl said. Far below her she could see the little lake, in full clearness, blinding white in sun, the island dark in the heart of it. "Not this time."

FATHERS' DAY
Nathaniel Benchley

George Adams finished his coffee, mashed out his cigarette in the saucer, and stood up. "I'm off," he said to his
wife as he went to the coat closet. "See you around six."

"Don't forget Bobby's school," she said.

Adams stopped, and looked at her. "What about it?"
he asked.

"They're having Fathers' Day," she said. "Remember?"

"Oh, my God," Adams said. He paused, then said hur-
riedly, "I can't make it. It's out of the question."

"You've got to," she said. "You missed it last year, and
he was terribly hurt. Just go for a few minutes, but you've
got to do it. I promised him I'd remind you."

Adams drew a deep breath and said nothing.

"Bobby said you could just come for English class,"
Eleanor went on. "Between twelve twenty and one. Please
don't let him down again."

"Well, I'll try," Adams said. "I'll make it if I can."

"It won't hurt you to do it. All the other fathers do."

"I'm sure they do," Adams said. He put on his hat and went out and rang for the elevator.

Eleanor came to the front door. "No excuses, now!" she said.

"I said I'd do it if I could," Adams replied. "That's all I can promise you."

Adams arrived at the school about twelve thirty, and an attendant at the door reached out to take his hat. "No, thanks," Adams said, clutching it firmly. "I'm just going to be a few minutes." He looked around and saw the cloakroom, piled high with hats and topcoats, and beyond that the auditorium, in which a number of men and boys were already having lunch. Maybe I'm too late, he thought hopefully. Maybe the classes are already over. To the attendant, he said, "Do you know where I'd find the sixth grade now? They're having English, I think."

"The office'll tell you," the attendant said. "Second floor."

Adams ascended a steel-and-concrete stairway to the second floor and, through the closed doors around him, heard the high, expressionless voices of reciting boys and the lower, softly precise voices of the teachers, and as he passed the open door of an empty room, he caught the smell of old wood and chalk dust and library paste. He found the office, and a middle-aged woman there directed him to a room on the floor above, and he went up and stood outside the door for a moment, listening. He could hear a teacher's voice, and the teacher was talking about the direct object and the main verb and the predicate adjective.

After hesitating a few seconds, Adams turned the knob and quietly opened the door. The first face he saw was that of his son, in the front row, and Bobby winked at him. Then Adams looked at the thin, dark-haired teacher, who seemed a surprisingly young man. He obviously had noticed Bobby's wink, and he smiled and said, "Mr. Adams." Adams tiptoed to the back of the room and joined about six other fathers, who were sitting in various attitudes of discomfort on a row of folding chairs. He recognized none of them, but they looked at him in a friendly way and he smiled at them, acknowledging the bond of uneasiness that held them momentarily together.

The teacher was diagramming a sentence on the blackboard, breaking it down into its component parts by means of straight and oblique lines, and Adams, looking at the diagram, realized that, if called upon, he would be hard put to it to separate the subject from the predicate, and he prayed that the teacher wouldn't suffer a fit of whimsy and call on the fathers. As it turned out, the students were well able to handle the problem, and Adams was gratified to hear his son give correct answers to two questions that were put to him. I'll be damned, Adams thought. I never got the impression he knew all that.

Then the problem was completed, and the teacher

glanced at the clock and said, "All right. Now we'll hear the compositions." He walked to the back of the room, sat down, and then looked around at a field of suddenly up-raised hands and said, "Go ahead, Getsinger. You go first."

A thin boy with wild blond hair and a red bow tie popped out of his seat and, carrying a sheet of paper, went to the front of the room and, in a fast, singsong voice, read, "He's So Understanding. I like my Dad because he's so understanding." Several of the boys turned in their seats and looked at one of the fathers and grinned as Getsinger went on, "When I ask Dad for a dime he says he'll settle for a nickel, and I say you can't get anything for a nickel any more and he says then he'll settle for six cents. Then pretty soon Mom calls and says that supper is ready, and the fight goes on in the dining room, and after a while Dad says he'll make it seven cents, and before supper is over I have my dime. That's why I say he's understanding."

Adams smiled in sympathy for Mr. Getsinger, and when the next boy got up and started off "Why I Like My Father," Adams realized with horror that all the compositions were going to be on the same subject, and he saw that his own son had a piece of paper on his desk and was waiting eagerly for his turn to read. The palms of Adams' hands became moist, and he looked at the clock, hoping that the time would run out before Bobby got a chance to recite. There was a great deal of laughter during the second boy's reading of his composition, and after he sat down, Adams looked at the clock again and saw that there were seven minutes left. Then the teacher looked around again, and five or six hands shot up, including Bobby's, and the teacher said, "All right—let's have Satterlee next," and Bobby took his hand down slowly, and Adams breathed more easily and kept his eyes riveted on the clock.

Satterlee, goaded by the laughter the previous student had received, read his composition with a mincing attempt to be comical, and he told how his father was unable to get any peace around the house, with his mother "chattering about the latest gossip" and his sister practicing the violin. It occurred to Adams that the compositions were nothing more than the children's impressions of their own home life, and the squirming and the nervous laughter from the fathers indicated that the observations were more acute than flattering. Adams tried to think what Bobby might say, and he could remember only things like the time he had docked Bobby's allowance for two weeks, for some offense he couldn't now recall, and the way he sometimes shouted at Bobby when he got too boisterous around the apartment, and the time Bobby had threatened to leave home because he had been forbidden to go to a vaudeville show—and the time he *had* left home because of a punishment Adams had given him. Adams thought also of the night he and his wife had had an argument, and how, the next day, Bobby had asked what "self-centered" meant, in reply to which Adams had told him it was none of his business. Then he remembered the time Bobby had been on a children's radio show and had announced that his household chores included getting out the ice for drinks, and when Adams asked him later why he had said it, Bobby had reminded him of one time Adams had asked him to bring an ice tray from the pantry into the living room. The memories they have, Adams thought—the diabolically selective memories.

Satterlee finished. The clock showed two minutes to one, and Adams wiped his hands on his trouser legs and gripped his hat, which was getting pulpy around the brim. Then Bobby's hand went up again, almost plaintively now, and the teacher said, "All right, Adams, you're on," and Bobby bobbed up and went to the front of the room.

Several of the boys turned and looked at Adams as Bobby began to read, but Adams was oblivious of everything except the stocky figure in front of the blackboard, whose tweed jacket looked too small for him and who was reading fast because the bell was about to ring. What Bobby read was a list of things that Adams had completely forgotten, or that had seemed of no great importance at the time, things like being allowed to stay up late to watch a fight, and being given an old fencing mask when there was no occasion for a gift (Adams had simply found it in a second-hand store and thought Bobby might like it), and having a model airplane made for him when he couldn't do it himself, and the time Adams had retrieved the ring from the subway grating. By the time Bobby concluded with "That's why he's O.K. in *my* book," Adams had recovered from his surprise and was beginning to feel embarrassed. Then the bell rang and class was dismissed, and Adams and the other fathers followed the boys out of the room.

Bobby was waiting for him in the corridor outside. "Hi," Bobby said. "You going now?"

"Yes," said Adams. "I'm afraid I've got to."

"O.K." Bobby turned and started away.

"Just a minute," Adams said, and Bobby stopped and looked back. Adams walked over to him and then hesitated a moment. "That was—ah—a good speech," he said.

"Thanks," said Bobby.

Adams started to say something else, but could think of nothing. "See you later," he finished, and quickly put on his hat and hurried down the stairs.

FLIGHT
Doris Lessing

Above the old man's head was the dovecote, a tall wire-netted shelf on stilts, full of strutting, preening birds. The sunlight broke on their gray breasts into small rainbows. His ears were lulled by their crooning; his hands stretched up toward his favorite, a homing pigeon, a young plump-bodied bird, which stood still when it saw him and cocked a shrewd bright eye.

"Pretty, pretty, pretty," he said, as he grasped the bird and drew it down, feeling the cold coral claws tighten around his finger. Content, he rested the bird lightly on his chest and leaned against a tree, gazing out beyond the dovecote into the landscape of a late afternoon. In folds and hollows of sunlight and shade, the dark red soil, which was broken into great dusty clods, stretched wide to a tall horizon. Trees marked the course of the valley; a stream of rich green grass the road.

His eyes traveled homeward along this road until he

saw his granddaughter swinging on the gate underneath a frangipani tree. Her hair fell down her back in a wave of sunlight; and her long bare legs repeated the angles of the frangipani stems, bare, shining brown stems among patterns of pale blossoms.

She was gazing past the pink flowers, past the railway cottage where they lived, along the road to the village.

His mood shifted. He deliberately held out his wrist for the bird to take flight, and caught it again at the moment it spread its wings. He felt the plump shape strive and strain under his fingers; and, in a sudden access of troubled spite, shut the bird into a small box and fastened the bolt. "Now you stay there," he muttered and turned his back on the shelf of birds. He moved warily along the hedge, stalking his granddaughter, who was now looped over the gate, her head loose on her arms, singing. The light happy sound mingled with the crooning of the birds, and his anger mounted.

"Hey!" he shouted, and saw her jump, look back, and abandon the gate. Her eyes veiled themselves, and she said in a pert, neutral voice, "Hullo, Grandad." Politely she moved toward him, after a lingering backward glance at the road.

"Waiting for Steven, hey?" he said, his fingers curling like claws into his palm.

"Any objection?" she asked lightly, refusing to look at him.

He confronted her, his eyes narrowed, shoulders hunched, tight in a hard knot of pain that included the preening birds, the sunlight, the flowers, herself. He said, "Think you're old enough to go courting, hey?"

The girl tossed her head at the old-fashioned phrase and sulked. "Oh, Grandad!"

"Think you want to leave home, hey? Think you can go running around the fields at night?"

Her smile made him see her, as he had every evening of this warm end-of-summer month, swinging hand in hand along the road to the village with that red-handed, red-throated, violent-bodied youth, the son of the postmaster. Misery went to his head and he shouted angrily: "I'll tell your mother!"

"Tell away!" she said, laughing, and went back to the gate.

He heard her singing, for him to hear:

> *"I've got you under my skin,*
> *I've got you deep in the heart of . . ."*

"Rubbish," he shouted. "Rubbish. Impudent little bit of rubbish!"

Growling under his breath, he turned toward the dovecote, which was his refuge from the house he shared with his daughter and her husband and their children. But now the house would be empty. Gone all the young girls with their laughter and their squabbling and their teasing. He would be left, uncherished and alone, with that square-fronted, clam-eyed woman, his daughter.

He stooped, muttering, before the dovecote, resenting the absorbed, cooing birds.

From the gate the girl shouted: "Go and tell! Go on, what are you waiting for?"

Obstinately he made his way to the house, with quick, pathetic, persistent glances of appeal back at her. But she never looked around. Her defiant but anxious young body stung him into love and repentance. He stopped. "But I never meant . . ." he muttered, waiting for her to turn and run to him. "I didn't mean . . ."

She did not turn. She had forgotten him. Along the road came the young man Steven, with something in his hand. A present for her? The old man stiffened as he watched the gate swing back and the couple embrace. In the brittle shadows of the frangipani tree his granddaughter, his darling, lay in the arms of the postmaster's son, and her hair flowed back over his shoulder.

"I see you!" shouted the old man spitefully. They did not move. He stumped into the little whitewashed house, hearing the wooden veranda creak angrily under his feet. His daughter was sewing in the front room, threading a needle held to the light.

He stopped again, looking back into the garden. The couple were now sauntering among the bushes, laughing. As he watched he saw the girl escape from the youth with a sudden mischievous movement and run off through the flowers with him in pursuit. He heard shouts, laughter, a scream, silence.

"But it's not like that at all," he muttered miserably. "It's not like that. Why can't you see? Running and giggling, and kissing and kissing. You'll come to something quite different."

He looked at his daughter with sardonic hatred, hating himself. They were caught and finished, both of them, but the girl was still running free.

"Can't you *see*?" he demanded of his invisible granddaughter, who was at that moment lying in the thick green grass with the postmaster's son.

His daughter looked at him and her eyebrows went up in tired forbearance.

"Put your birds to bed?" she asked, humoring him.

"Lucy," he said urgently. "Lucy. . . ."

"Well, what is it now?"

"She's in the garden with Steven."

"Now you just sit down and have your tea."

He stumped his feet alternately, thump, thump, on the hollow wooden floor and shouted: "She'll marry him. I'm telling you, she'll be marrying him next!"

His daughter rose swiftly, brought him a cup, set him a plate.

"I don't want any tea. I don't want it, I tell you."

"Now, now," she crooned. "What's wrong with it? Why not?"

"She's eighteen. Eighteen!"

"I was married at seventeen, and I never regretted it."

"Liar," he said. "Liar. Then you should regret it. Why do you make your girls marry? It's you who do it. What do you do it for? Why?"

"The other three have done fine. They've three fine husbands. Why not Alice?"

"She's the last," he mourned. "Can't we keep her a bit longer?"

"Come, now, Dad. She'll be down the road, that's all. She'll be here every day to see you."

"But it's not the same." He thought of the other three girls, transformed inside a few months from charming, petulant, spoiled children into serious young matrons.

"You never did like it when we married," she said. "Why not? Every time, it's the same. When I got married you made me feel like it was something wrong. And my girls the same. You get them all crying and miserable the way you go on. Leave Alice alone. She's happy." She sighed, letting her eyes linger on the sunlit garden. "She'll marry next month. There's no reason to wait."

"You've said they can marry?" he said incredulously.

"Yes, Dad. Why not?" she said coldly and took up her sewing.

His eyes stung, and he went out on to the veranda. Wet spread down over his chin, and he took out a handkerchief and mopped his whole face. The garden was empty.

From around the corner came the young couple; but their faces were no longer set against him. On the wrist of the postmaster's son balanced a young pigeon, the light gleaming on its breast.

"For me?" said the old man, letting the drops shake off his chin. "For me?"

"Do you like it?" The girl grabbed his hand and swung on it. "It's for you, Grandad. Steven brought it for you." They hung about him, affectionate, concerned, trying to charm away his wet eyes and his misery. They took his arms and directed him to the shelf of birds, one on each side, enclosing him, petting him, saying wordlessly that nothing would be changed, nothing could change, and that they would be with him always. The bird was proof of it, they said, from their lying happy eyes, as they thrust it on him. "There, Grandad, it's yours. It's for you."

They watched him as he held it on his wrist, stroking its soft, sun-warmed back, watching the wings lift and balance.

"You must shut it up for a bit," said the girl intimately, "until it knows this is its home."

"Teach your grandmother to suck eggs," growled the old man.

Released by his half-deliberate anger, they fell back, laughing at him. "We're glad you like it." They moved off, now serious and full of purpose, to the gate, where they hung, backs to him, talking quietly. More than anything could, their grown-up seriousness shut him out, making him alone; also, it quietened him, took the sting out of their tumbling like puppies on the grass. They had forgotten him again. Well, so they should, the old man reassured himself, feeling his throat clotted with tears, his lips trembling. He held the new bird to his face, for the caress of its silken feathers. Then he shut it in a box and took out his favorite.

"*Now* you can go," he said aloud. He held it poised, ready for flight, while he looked down the garden toward the boy and the girl. Then, clenched in the pain of loss, he lifted the bird on his wrist and watched it soar. A whirr and a spatter of wings, and a cloud of birds rose into the evening from the dovecote.

At the gate Alice and Steven forgot their talk and watched the birds.

On the veranda, that woman, his daughter, stood gazing, her eyes shaded with a hand that still held her sewing.

It seemed to the old man that the whole afternoon had stilled to watch his gesture of self-command, that even the leaves of the trees had stopped shaking.

Dry-eyed and calm, he let his hands fall to his sides and stood erect, staring up into the sky.

The cloud of shining silver birds flew up and up, with a shrill cleaving of wings, over the dark ploughed land and the darker belts of trees and the bright folds of grass, until they floated high in the sunlight, like a cloud of motes of dust.

They wheeled in a wide circle, tilting their wings so there was flash after flash of light, and one after another they dropped from the sunshine of the upper sky to shadow, one after another, returning to the shadowed earth over trees and grass and field, returning to the valley and the shelter of night.

The garden was all a fluster and a flurry of returning birds. Then silence, and the sky was empty.

The old man turned, slowly, taking his time; he lifted his eyes to smile proudly down the garden at his grand-daughter. She was staring at him. She did not smile. She was wide-eyed and pale in the cold shadow, and he saw the tears run shivering off her face.

OTHER PAPERBACK ORIGINALS